Collar Me

M.G. Cruickshank

Wunderhaus Press
New York, NY

Wunderhaus Press
New York, NY
wunderhauspress@gmail.com

Publisher's Note: This is a work of fiction. Names, characters, places, and incidents are a product of the author's imagination. Locales and public names are sometimes used for atmospheric purposes. Any resemblance to actual people, living or dead, or to businesses, companies, events, institutions, or locales is completely coincidental.

Book Layout ©2021 BookDesignTemplates.com

Collar Me/ M.G. Cruickshank. ~ 1st ed.
Paperback Edition: ISBN 978-1-7365635-0-2
Hardcover Edition: ISBN 978-1-7365635-1-0
EPUB Edition: ISBN 978-1-7365635-2-6
Mobipocket Edition: ISBN 978-1-7365635-3-3

Contents

This book is dedicated to M.S. who has been with me through thick and thin...forever...

Chapter 1

Another photo shoot finished, Georgia sat naked at her computer, sipped a coffee and prepared to light a cigarette. She twirled a strand of frosted hair with her forefinger while idly scrolling through the Craigslist help wanted ads: dog walker, assistant to anybody, gal Friday. She applied to a couple of positions out of boredom, then clicked on the personals, going immediately to BDSM. Within minutes, she landed on Mistress Chunxx's website: "Learn the exotic art of Bondage, Discipline and Sadomasochism. Become a dominatrix."

There it is, she thought to herself, *right where Richard said it would be.* Georgia filled out the form, including her body type and personality, and clicked send. She received a response almost immediately.

"This is Mistress Chunxx. You are formally invited to attend our free introductory BDSM seminar. Visit us and walk on the wild side. Learn the lucrative profession of dominating the rich and powerful." Her eyes grew wide in anticipation of the prospect.

"Cool," she mumbled, "Richard will be so proud of me, and maybe I can surprise him with some new moves."

Now connected with purpose, Georgia had meaning in her life, or at least something to look forward to. "I could actually make a living at this," she fantasized. Listening to Richard talk about Chunxx and devouring those explicit photographs on the site, she thought to herself, *this is my world...these are my people. They'll understand me like nobody else.*

Photos, mostly of her, were scattered around her apartment, along with a few recent downloads from the Mistress Chunxx website, pictures of Richard tied up and having the crap pounded out him. Georgia collected them and slipped them into a desk drawer. Stupid, boring Harry was coming over for dinner and she certainly wouldn't want him finding any incriminating evidence.

What the fuck am I going to do with him, she wondered. He's just a habit at this point. Oh well, at least I can get fucked a few more times a week, when Richard's unavailable. He's kind and he always pays for dinner. Sure, Harry's a perv—well not a pro like Richard—but I'm so used to him and so over him. Her mood darkened as she considered another meal at home with Harry.

He's so predictable...he goes down on me and I cum and then I put his cock in me and he cums and then we watch TV and I pass out and he goes home.

An hour later, predictably on schedule, her door opened. Harry removed his key from the lock and walked in smiling. He carried a grocery bag with a freshly cooked rotisserie chicken and some premade salads.

And here he is, she thought. Boring.

At the tail end of their dinner, the remaining chicken and salad sat on the table. Georgia never ate much, preferring to drink her dinner. Her plate of food sat largely untouched. She handed him some of her most recent photos and he looked them over, giving the kindest criticism he could muster. Georgia tossed down another white wine, alone. Harry rarely drank more than a sip or two of anything alcoholic. Her consumption, on the other hand, more than compensated for his abstinence.

"Nice," he lied, "And why are they all naked?"

Though they would be considered bland from any artistic standpoint, the images in front of him brought on a surge of arousal. He looked to her for some response and met a blank gaze. Remaining highly aroused, he continued to look through the stack of photos. Georgia made no comment

"Well anyway your body looks great." Still nothing from Georgia. "Why don't you try some other stuff? Other poses, curled up, back to the camera. You know, mix things up."

Together for nine years, the mere sound of this woman's voice on the telephone still sent electricity down his spine, into his solar plexus, slowing the blood flow to a very specific region, resulting in a subsequent penile tumescence. He was hard as a rock. Seeing Georgia exhibit her body—openly, blatantly, wantonly in a photograph, for the world to look at, took his breath away. Maintaining an outward cool, he admired what used to be a more than ample bush, now carefully manicured and maintained by his own skillful hand.

He reworked their ritual in his head: using a combination of electric hair clippers, scissors, and razors with soft, foamy shaving cream, wiping away any extra pubic hair with a warm washcloth—repeatedly, obsessively shaving the delicate areas, flipping her over on her hard tummy to make sure that every hair from the marvelous pink anal sphincter was removed. Parting those tight cloves a twelve year old Swedish boy could own; cleaning with the warm, white wash cloth, then rinsing again—perfectly clean—then testing for a remaining nib or two of hair with a tongue working its way around each side, then down between, to the hot, smooth, brown eye...

Georgia's voice pulled him out of the reverie. "I like the classic pose. You know...straightforward and, well, classy."

They took their plates and stacked them in the sink. Georgia returned to the table and filled her wine glass, almost to the brim, as Harry brewed some tea. She continued to drink alone, seemingly lost in a private stupor.

"Are you going to continue with this series?" he asked.

"Which series?" She was somewhere else, forgetting that she was at the table, supposedly talking with her boyfriend.

"The classic nudes."

"Oh, I don't know. I need something...something exciting to do, Harry," she responded, not really caring.

"Like what? Like skydiving? Or maybe deep sea fishing. River dance?" he said, a bit sarcastically.

"Like...ummm, maybe, modeling—or assistant to a billionaire in Monaco?" She lobbed his bit of sarcasm back as she talked slowly—the only sign that she was getting drunk.

Maybe I should tell Harry about my idea, Georgia ruminated. In a flash, she felt like revealing her BDSM ambitions, but thought better of it. It would ruin the excitement, the taboo, the titillation, the betrayal that so turned her on and gave her purpose, so lacking in the rest of her life.

"Anything like that online? Have you been looking online?" The question seemed like it caught Georgia slightly off guard, snapping her back to the moment.

"Yeah, no, nothing that suits me. I dunno...dog walking? At least I could have some control."

Harry watched Georgia gather her composure, stonewalling him—one of her specialties. "Well maybe," he laughed.

The desire to tell him welled up in her again. She wanted him to know everything she'd been up to. Actually, her affair with Richard Lipschitz might be very cool if she could include another man. Why not Harry? She would love to watch her two male lovers fuck in all ways possible, then beat the crap out of each other. The mere thought filled her corpus cavernosum with hot red blood. No, that would ruin the excitement, the taboo, the titillation, the betrayal that so turned her on.

She finished the entire bottle of white wine and was not the least bit inebriated. Harry slid next to her and seductively kissed her neck. She allowed it, but didn't reciprocate. He removed her sweater and kissed her breasts while she studiously ignored him. She felt him run a hand down the small of her back, past the waistband of her black, skintight, Lululemon workout pants. Fingers rested briefly on her coccyx, then parted the tight cloves of her ass and continued sneaking down to the edge of her hot, tan, salty asshole.

Harry's actions were beginning to have an effect, whether she wanted them to or not but, as if on schedule, the phone rang. It was Richard's new ringtone, a cheesy electronic version of Mozart's piano sonata #16 in C major. Georgia nonchalantly stood and pulled her pants back up, destroying all of Harry's painstaking work that had exposed that perfect crack. She answered the phone, walking with it into the bedroom.

"Hi... no, I have *company*." Georgia began to laugh, as though Harry wasn't even in the apartment. "I was thinking about being a dog walker. Yes, I'm serious...a dog walker. Why not? I love dogs." She paused, listening to the other side of the conversation. "Yes, I do. How would you know? What?" She laughed, "You're kidding. Who knows, I'm not sure," she giggled.

There was a longer pause on her side of the conversation before she spoke again, this time in a more serious tone. "Yeah, but do you think I could? But the dog walking thing. Yeah. Okay. Hey I took some photos I like... sure... maybe... really?" Finally, she laughed and quietly said, "See you tomorrow."

Georgia returned to the kitchen table where Harry sat studying her photographs, but not really paying any attention to them. It was easy to tell he'd been listening to the call. Before he could ask, she blurted, "Listen, I'm not feeling well. I have to go to a football game tomorrow morning with some friends. You gotta go now. I need to get some sleep. I have to go to bed." She put on her best sleepy face, though she was actually quite energized by the idea of doing something completely off her radar with Richard. She wondered what other perv friends he might bring along.

"Oh, sorry you're not well. What's wrong?" Harry asked, offering his best fake concern. "Who was that on the phone?"

"That was Becky Jackson," she said as she joined him on the couch and sidled closer. "She and some of her posse have an extra ticket and are taking me to a football game tomorrow. And why so nosy? Here, can you massage my neck?" She requested, trying to subvert Harry's inquiry.

Harry began to massage her. "Football?" he asked, his hands moving lower, down toward her backside once again.

"Yeah, I like football," she lied.

"Since when?"

"Since now," Georgia stated, defiant.

Resting his head on her shoulder, eyes closed, Harry reflected back a couple of months to one of Becky Jackson's *cavalcade of ghouls* parties. A successful real estate agent, and a certified freak, Becky threw a monthly soirée for all the crazies she'd been collecting over the years, with many new faces at every event. Her large Upper West Side duplex was a swarm of stoned and drunken artists, poets, men in suits, and miscreants from the financial world—all smoking, eating Chinese, talking over one another, yelling and laughing, getting more and more drunk. Becky was on the phone, in his recollection, escalating an argument with some take-out person at a restaurant.

"What the fuck? You think I care that you're a fucking delivery guy? You're an asshole anyway. Why don't you go back to where you came from? Idiot!" she screamed into the receiver. She laughed, "Yeah, real funny, creep! I love you too. Now leave me-alone. I just want some food you jerk-chicken-shit-Chinaman!" she yelled into the phone and then sobbed, "Why can't you just be nice?" Her mood turned on a dime to escalating anger. "Who, me?" He heard her pause, and then scream, "Fuck off, brutal alien!" She threw the phone across the room and laughed hysterically. Becky was off her meds.

Everyone in the crammed living room toasted her and then raised a glass to every jerk-chicken-shit-Chinaman in Manhattan.

Harry was shooting all this with his video camera, having been asked by Becky to document the evening. He could see that Georgia was fascinated by Becky and her crazy antics. Harry panned around the room, getting extreme close-ups of the weirdoes Becky picked up all over town. By the door, he caught a late-comer to the party. The guy sidled in and headed directly to the bar and the hard liquor. Georgia stood with her back to him, fixing herself another vodka martini. Harry filmed the guy checking her out from behind, noting her thin legs and petite, tight ass encased in black stretch pants and then, in turn, her pinched, sad, WASPy expression.

Harry continued shooting from the other side of the room, surrounded by loud chit-chat and sloppy, inebriated laughter. He had no way to eavesdrop and no clue that what he was witnessing would profoundly change three people's lives forever.

Georgia was mining the crowd when she sensed a gaze in her direction and turned around. Someone new raised his eyes to her face and gave her a broad, whited-toothed smile. She gave him the once over, noted his short stumpy fingers, his gold and diamond pinky ring, his darkly tanned face, his gold Rolex watch, yellow neck tie and black business suit. The guy was pretty overweight, but maybe he had some money.

"Got another one of those," he asked, nodding toward the martini.

"Coming right up, big boy," she said, always the flirt—a drunken, horny coquette. She turned and made a second drink.

When she turned back to hand him his drink, she noticed her new friend scan the room. He seemed to be scrutinizing all the women and passing over the men with a quick glance, before returning his attention to her.

"Nice ass," he said, under his breath.

"Excuse me, I beg your pardon?" Georgia demanded, pretending indignation.

"I said 'nice eyes'," he winked. Knowing the most available, vulnerable, and easiest target in the room was directly in front of him.

Georgia laughed, "You did not, you said 'nice ass'."

"No I didn't. Really! Okay, I did. You have a nice ass. Does it bother you that I commented on that fact?" he asked, honestly. Georgia was intrigued and flattered, in spite of herself.

"You're a doll. You're beautiful," he continued, all charm. "Do you believe in love at first sight? Allow me to introduce myself, my name is Richard. Richard Lipschitz." He took a healthy swig of his martini.

"Nice to meet you, Richard Lipschitz," she replied, and batted her eyes. "Need a refill? You're getting low there. By the way I have a boyfriend."

They smiled and clinked glasses, toasting her boyfriend. Georgia refilled his glass. "Yeah? Oh really?" Lipschitz asked.

"Yeah. And my name is Georgia, by the way. Nice to meet you." They locked eyes, both playing the same game.

Meanwhile, Harry panned around the room with his camera on a tripod, pulling in quite close with a telephoto lens. His subjects were getting extremely smashed. *Just look at these mindless fools, this sea of human scum*

drooling over one another; slobbering, sloppy, slime sucking freaks returned to Georgia, his lens focused extremely tight on her face as she knocked down another vodka martini, and then mixed another for the ape she was talking to. This fat slob is wearing a rug, colored with black shoe polish...what a dick, he thought. He pulled the shot back a little so they were both in frame, and settled in to watch the silent show.

He wasn't often possessive. In fact, he enjoyed the flirtation he witnessed through his camera. Sometimes he slightly, or even intensely, despised Georgia. And yet, at the same time, he enjoyed his jealousy and anger when it came to her. It was hot, for one, and the sex was much better when you disliked your partner somewhat. At least, this was one of his pet theories.

So, spying on his girlfriend being hit on by a professional sleazebag in such an over the top ridiculous way, pumped adrenaline into his guts. And witnessing someone he trusted, or at least pretended to trust, excited him inexplicably. Thinking about it, he supposed he never actually trusted her—or even particularly liked her consistently... And, being fairly sure that she felt the same way toward him, served both their purposes. In many ways, through their mutual disrespect and dislike for each other, they were emotional twins. He didn't really care about Georgia's behavior, or so he thought. After all, what was betrayal in a non-trust relationship? What was truly exciting was that what he was witnessing made it crystal clear: that he could, with pleasure and without remorse, strangle and mutilate his male adversary. As Harry's body filled with adrenalin, his brain calmed and focused on the ensuing fight. He was ready to tear an adversary to shreds: eye gouging, ear ripping face chewing. There would be little left of his mortal enemy. Harry was a caveman protecting his property and territory; a simple instinct, his right and duty as the offspring of knuckle-dragging cretins. *This was the stuff of life*, he thought.

Georgia twisted away from his hopeful, groping, grip. She disappeared into to her bedroom without looking back.

"Now good night, Harry," she called, a stern edge in her voice.

Suspicious, lying on her couch, wondering what was going on, descending into that familiar sadness of being rejected, he contemplated jumping out the window. He got up and walked to the sill.

Something seemed off, way off this time. Abandonment triggered fear and rage in him. His control was slipping; he could feel it draining like blood.

"GOOD NIGHT," demanded Georgia again, through the closed door, distant and colder than ever.

Chapter 2

Harry Waldheim's Journal

Do you know what it's like to get punched in the face? It doesn't actually hurt. The blow occurs almost in slow motion, and then in an instant warm blood rushes to the surface of the skin at the point of impact. It almost feels good. If you're me, you don't flinch or blink or pause, or overtly react at all. You stare down the old man, demanding another shot. He gives it, this time on the other cheek. Then a few more shots. The beating strengthens your resolve. None of this hurts, but your ears are ringing and you can barely hear. You internalize your hatred, and as the bully stumbles out of the room, you realize that you've just slammed him in the balls. He will never hit you again after this. He won't speak to you for three weeks. You are thirteen years old.

Chapter 3

He pulled at and caught a brief memory from a time long ago, a moment of joy and bliss... for a few seconds, he was once again a young boy immersed in nature.... The cicadas are in full force: scraping wings, metal against metal, grinding-friction, the droning throat songs of nomads and monks, loud monotones mesmerize every molecule of flora and fauna. It's hot and humid—high noon. Shafts of August sunlight seep past dense canopies of sugar maples, ash, oak and white pine, illuminating small patches of ground. Soft steam lifts from deep green moss and fern: the forest floor. Eight-year-old blond-haired, blue-eyed Harry Waldheim, the rolled up cuffs of his jeans filled with leaves and crap, his filthy, white tee-shirt (a hand-me-down from an older cousin) is now ripped as he runs wild through the woods he thinks of as his own. The air is cooler and moist beneath the trees, as he hops over moss-covered logs half buried in dark muck, sinking to his ankles. He splashes down the brook—clear and fresh—to the pond. He puts his hand in the water and takes a sip.

He spies a leopard frog half-hidden in a safe covering of bright green algae, as a Pileated Woodpecker swoops by, like a pterodactyl, diving to her nest in a hollow tree to feed her squawking brood high above. Harry is feral, as only an eight-year-old can be. He pauses briefly, to pee, gazing upward as a gentle wind moves the canopy of green leaves. For a brief moment all of nature speaks to him. He is frozen in time as the cicadas, the woodpeckers, and a distant hermit thrush harmonize with the gentle stirring of trees. He blinks, zips his fly, and is off again, dashing and leaping, branches hitting the forearms he holds up to protect his face. He is zigzagging toward his secret place made of twigs and branches, covered with leaves and moss. He stops abruptly at his destination, the base of the tallest white pine in the world...his climbing tree. Harry is invisible, immersed in nature where nobody can find him, ever.

In the absolute middle of America an extremely modest cape cod style tract home was built on once pristine and fertile farmland surrounded by a very old forest. It was one of at least 100 brand new houses packed on either side of the tar and gravel road recently christened *Harmon Glen*. With no regard for variation, each house was built the same: two bedrooms, one bathroom, a living room, eat in kitchen, attic, basement and a one car garage tacked onto the left side. There were no trees, no lawns, just beige sand smoothly bulldozed around each identical new home. Eventually, people planted grass and symmetrically placed shrubs, trying to reduce the sterile feel of the neighborhood. Some homemakers planted petunias and marigolds, too, for rare hints of color.

Harry was seven when he moved to 38 Hawthorn Glen. A year later he was sharing his bedroom with a new baby brother, but he soon moved up into the tiny attic, alone at last once more. It was an uninsulated, bare wood frame, smelling of pine pitch and creosote, hardly inhabitable, but at least it was a few layers of sheetrock and floor board away from the screaming newborn and bickering parents.

On most nights, as eight-year-old Harry lay awake in bed, the thin filtered sounds of canned laughter, along with the two adults chuckling on cue in the living room downstairs, would rise up through the ceiling into his provisional attic bedroom. And, on most nights, the boy would silently creep down the stairs in his pajamas, homemade cardboard periscope in hand, and peek around the corner. The TV and a couch were the only pieces of furniture in the tiny beige living room, illuminated by the steadily flickering cathode rays. His parents, oblivious to their son hiding on the stairs, would puff cigarettes, sip from cans of beer, and laugh drunkenly at the crass sitcom on TV. Sometimes he would watch them groping, feeling and probing each other in escalating intensity, as they pretended to watch *The Dick Van Dyke Show* or *I Love Lucy* or *Candid Camera*.

That night, he saw his mom's pocket book open and hanging on the door a few feet away from him. Without thinking, he reached inside, opened her wallet and pulled out all the money—two twenties and five ones—then snuck back upstairs to his bedroom and fell fast asleep.

He woke later to rough shaking and the sensation that his hair was being pulled out by the roots. He opened his eyes to his parents' angry faces close to his own.

"Wake up you goddamn thief!" His mother had him by the shoulders and was shaking him and pulling his hair with drunken, angry rage. She stepped back, hands on hips, hair in curlers, a cigarette in one hand and the wad of cash in the other.

"And what's this? What do you think you're doing? You think you're smarter than we are? There are two of us and one of you." His father grabbed him by the hair again, "Sneaky kid. You're a bad seed, boy. We'll deal with this in the morning," he said, pulling Harry closer to his face by the boy's hair, bloodshot eyes staring, Harry could smell beer, cigarettes, a slight whiff of deodorant, and an odd fish-like odor.

"This is the last time you're EVER going to pull something like this. You are not growing up under this roof a thief or a sneak or a juvenile delinquent you...shit for brains!" he barked.

When they were gone, Harry sat up in his bed and looked out the window, through the screen. A persistent gypsy moth failed in its attempt to get in, but continued tapping repeatedly. The night was filled with the sounds of crickets, the sky filled with stars. A crescent moon peeked from behind a single altostratus cloud. He took the screen out and considered running away, but fell back into his bed and covered his head with a pillow. He listened to the muffled night sounds of the crickets and a whippoorwill crescendo around him as he escaped into deep slumber.

The next morning Harry thought that maybe being busted last night was only a dream. He climbed down the stairs from his room in the attic and entered the kitchen. His father looked up from his coffee, newspaper and cigarette.

"Put your books down now and meet me in the basement. No breakfast. No school," he commanded. "Now move. You heard me. Move."

Slowly and obediently, Harry set his books on the kitchen table. He looked up to see his mother sitting in silence, smoking a cigarette, drinking a cup of coffee, staring out the window. He opened the basement door then closed and silently locked it behind him and walked down into the dark.

The basement had been "fixed up" with paneling and furnished with an old piano, a ping-pong table and a few chairs from the old kitchen set. A slapped-together bar, specially constructed for a New Year's Eve party a couple of years earlier, stood cramped in a corner. A homemade "Happy New Year" sign remained taped above it. On the ping-pong table were his father's special implements: a dark brown leather belt, a large hair brush, and an old solid oak yardstick. The room was dark except for a few rays of filtered sunlight that angled through two small basement windows.

Quietly, Harry slid a chair from the old kitchen set beneath one of the small windows. He unlatched and pushed it open, just barely squeezing his small frame out. As soon as he was free of the window, he hightailed it into the woods, making a bee line for his secret place.

Within minutes, Harry Waldheim, wearing his school clothes, sat cross-legged in his primitive hut, smoking a cigarette stolen from his mother, and nervously thumbed through a comic book. Magazines, books, a roll of toilet paper and one mostly torn up Playboy littered the floor. He built a fire, using an entire pack of matches to get it lit and then tossed all the magazines, Playboy on top, into the flames. He took a picture of the burning magazine with his little plastic box camera and then threw it into his knapsack. The fort caught fire as Harry scampered to the top of the giant white pine...his sanctuary and only friend in the world.

Chapter 4

Harry Waldheim's Journal

When you get shoved out of a pipe and land on your head, the parts of you that survive are rarely connected. Pretending becomes a way of life; hiding those voids, at least from yourself, is something you just have to do. The world knows what you're up to though, and it will try with all its might to break you down, to expose the empty spaces. It wants to rip you to shreds and tread upon the scraps; you will be the fodder and food of the chosen few. They know who you are and need you to be in your place and under their heel...

Chapter 5

Georgia and Harry mostly just co-existed and tolerated one another, always with their eyes open for some painless exit. And, at least for Harry, the sex was great, and it did satisfy more than just his physical needs. But the strongest attraction, maybe even addiction, was to the pain; a familiar disemboweling that only fear, anger and hatred could conjure.

There was always the fear of potential abandonment implied by their mutual lack of commitment and emotional distance. Theirs was an odd combination of trust and distrust, never consistent, which may have been fuel to their sexual fire while just as much the extinguisher. Their attraction was their addiction to the emotional pain that they caused in one another. Abandonment was something they both grew up with and was now their comfort zone, as they constantly abandoned each other in all sorts of complicated ways.

Watching Georgia through his lens, quite drunk, on the make, he could almost dream this betrayal. It brought the sober Harry in an instant back to a very familiar place. That feeling of rejection and abandonment was quite, unquestionably, his home.

He remembered sitting at the kitchen table, doing homework. He was, maybe, twelve. His mother and one of her idiotic girlfriends were drinking coffee and talking about god-knows-what. And then she said it.

"Having children is like making pancakes," with a gesture to her firstborn, Harry. "You always throw the first one away."

Harry snapped out of his memory. To the already suspicious and paranoid Harry, Georgia seemed more off than usual. She was up to something. This was not the normal passive aggressive, bad vibe, crabby Georgia Harry had grown accustomed to. His instincts, sharpened from years of abuse and betrayal by the cretins that had so rudely ushered him into the world, were screaming at him to run, to hide, to protect himself from danger. *Kill or be killed sad vulnerable child. It's time for you to hide!*

"Fuck me!" He yelled, out into the dark cacophony of the city from thirty-four floors up. There was no response.

He threw his jacket over his shoulder, and without saying goodbye, he quietly closed her door and walked down the hallway toward the elevator. The smells of boiled cabbage and chicken stock filled the drab corridor, and he wondered—as he had before—if he would ever return to this institutional prison of painted metal doors, beige interiors, and wall-to-wall nylon carpet. He stepped into the elevator. Fortunately it was empty. He didn't care to have the annoyance of riding with one of the many fat old bags and their overweight, pampered mutts down that slow journey from the thirty-fourth floor. The stench of that building, he recalled as it punished his olfactory senses, triggering old emotions and memories of the hundreds of times he'd traveled through this lobby, past the disgruntled night doorman, and out into the busy streets of Manhattan.

Happiness, having been the exception, far more than the rule, depressed for most of his life, with first thoughts of suicide at age eight, having been accused of uncommitted crimes, pushed around, tortured and never understood, he knew it had hit him. So familiar, this slowing way down: each leg a five hundred pound lifeless slab of blubber, the air a thick, poisonous soup, breathing almost impossible, and arms so weak they could barely lift a scrap of tissue paper. Twenty blocks from home seemed like light years away, and time had almost stopped to match his pace. His eyes surveyed every detail of the grubby streets, which, only a few hours ago were a packed and teaming melting pot but were now almost empty.

Harry, one agonizing step at a time, used every ounce of will power he could muster and shuffled past several shopping carts piled with bags lashed to bags, filled with cans and scraps of anything that could be sold for a few pennies. Closer now, he realized the carts sheltered a soot-covered, naked couple camped on a few scraps of cardboard. Oblivious, without shame, she was on her back, guiding her partner's cock in and out of her mouth while he, on his knees, had his head buried between her legs, hands cupping her ample hindquarters—a grime-encrusted sack of flesh stuffed with large curd cottage cheese. Harry stood mutely, watching...surveilling...slowly...so slow...so tired of his mortal coil.

The couple grunted, separated briefly, and stared blankly back at the mute carcass of Harry as he sluggishly turned to leave.

"You owe us a hundred bucks!" whined the nasally male junky addict. "No free shows in this fuckin' town!"

Harry continued his shuffle homeward as the guy's demands diminished into the background of sirens and nocturnal garbage trucks grinding up the day's flotsam and jetsam.

"Give me a fuckin' cigarette, at least!" the last grumble barely audible with Harry now almost block away. He sloughed past a crater, gouged from the street pavement, which revealed the rusted veins of rotting city infrastructure. Steam blasted from a frail cylinder as swarthy workers stood around dumbly, wondering what to do next. Pausing, his eyes pulled in every detail like a high-speed camera, his inhales reduced to a few deep breaths per minute. A clear brain filled with paralyzing cortisol was telling him to die. If only he had the strength to find a rope, tie a noose and hang himself. But where? Too depressed to answer that question, he ever so slowly continued to drag his sorry ass the ten remaining blocks home through empty streets, past cold walls of steel and glass and concrete.

"Fuck, shit, piss!" The scream came from nowhere. Probably some Tourette's Syndrome lunatic, Harry thought. But it snapped him slightly out of his obsessive stupor.

Almost home now, a flock of punk yuppies—all blue blazers-khakis-sockless in Guccis, insouciant, dead drunk, staggered arm-in-arm—looked on as one of their own convulsed, doubling over, and blasted vomit onto the sidewalk.

Raised to be a bottom feeder, Harry Waldheim learned to pick through the trash to find what little nourishment was available. This sorrow has kept him alive, barely; unaware of the gravitational pull hurling him through his life, through this feted maze of bowels and ultimately

regurgitating him back into the ecosystem that created this sad little being.

Harry, almost silently, hummed his favorite blues mantra, finally
reaching home.

> *Ain't got no mamma*
> *She dead and gone*
> *Ain't got no poppa*
> *Was never known*
> *Ain't got no-body*
> *Ain't got no friends*
> *All I got....be my dyin' end..*
> > *Blind Mellon Waldheim*

Chapter 6

A week before Harry discovered Georgia's secret life

Georgia Pendleton, lay under Harry, in the missionary position. Her eyes were closed, giving her long, beautiful lashes a sense of elegance. She was possessed of a small, slightly turned up, Anglo-Saxon nose and tight thin lips that were slowly opening and closing with deep rhythmic breaths. A slight scowl formed marionette lines and those tiny, parallel vertical creases across her upper lip, perhaps a result of too many cigarettes or too much sun, regardless, they betrayed her otherwise youthful body. Her deep steady breathing intensified as she shifted and moved.

A 43-year-old Harry Waldheim, zoomed his video camera in for an extreme close up; a student of form, shape, movement, color, texture, chiaroscuro, not to mention the aesthetics of explicit sexuality, he watched Georgia's face in the flip out monitor. The image was grainy as the camera was set for low light record mode. Strands of bleached blonde hair seemed to blow in the wind as she turned her head from side to side. He zoomed back slightly, revealing slender naked shoulders, and collar bones defining the lower frame of the moving image. She breathed deeply, in and out, as Harry panned slowly downward, lingering and hovering on those, perhaps too-perfect, too-round, too-solid orbs of flesh-covered silicone. Sweet nipples, pale pink hardened nubs, rode sensually atop their newly enhanced domain. Slowly the camera continued downward, past her tight, almost child-like, abdomen and then lower, to where Harry and Georgia were connected, their hot, moist, pink flesh forming a sexual union. Rolling over, he was on his back now, as she rode him like a slow-motion rodeo bull. Her left hand pressed past a freshly waxed mons pubis, labia minora open wide; forefinger set firmly on her hardened clitoral knob. Her other arm clutched his knee; a folded cradle supported Georgia as she did most of the work, grinding with increasingly intense ferocity.

She was turned on by her own exhibitionism and he, a consummate voyeur, loved looking at everything through a lens. She began the slow crescendo toward her orgasm as his breathing became longer, deeper, and more intense. They were getting closer and closer; slowly, she first, silently gyrating, continued the deep, silent, determined grind, in her own world. He was equally unemotional and detached, as he observed her orgasm and faked his own. Tenderly, they slid apart. He set the camera down haphazardly, next to the bed, as he and Georgia softly spooned, her post coital endorphins sinking them into an affectionate bliss.

"Are you comfortable?" he asked.

"Mmmmmm...yeahhhh."

They kissed. "Want to watch a movie?"

"Okay...do you have Blue Velvet?" whispered Harry.

"Think so, actually...let me see."

She reached over and grabbed a book full of DVDs and began to thumb through it. "Isabella is so cool, especially in that. I would love to be her."

Turning toward her, Harry said, "I'm getting a little hungry. What about you?"

"Can I boil you an egg...or how about some grapes?" She reached over and gave him a little kiss.

Harry's mobile phone rang. He grabbed it from the nightstand and Glanced at the caller ID; it was his mother. He ignored it and waited for the ding of a message, which never came. "Whenever I visit them," he mused, "I want to hang myself there, on their property, so that they find me dead, hanging from a light fixture, or a door knob, or in their cellar, or garage, or from a tree in the back yard. That would serve them right, he thought.

He returned his gaze to Georgia, and gently cradled her head in his two large hands, softly caressed her ears and tenderly swept over erogenous zones discovered years ago. He was still highly charged. He pulled her face closer, and their tongues passed like slithering snakes, their heat all-consuming. Soon they were at it again, as the camera remained on, in record mode, a blurry close up of their pink naked bodies writhing once again played out on the tiny screen.

Georgia left while Harry was in the shower. She locked the door after her with the key he had given her nine years ago. It was their habit that they never slept together, but they always checked in by phone several times a day. They had the perfect relationship, pretended Harry, lots of space, yet lots of trust.

Just past 40, Georgia was quite beautiful, with a petite, athletic body. She could do a handstand, remaining absolutely rigid, and then move into a perfect upside down split and pike to the floor. She would sometimes do this naked, in front of Harry, never ceasing to amaze him with her athletic prowess, sexual appetite, and her ability to tease. The irony of her normal frowning expression and her sad eyes wasn't lost on him. She carried an ancient sadness, a feeling that she was adrift at sea, still, she was always the little cocktease.

In her apartment at 1011 Park Avenue, once occupied by her great aunt on her father's side, a camera was set up on a tripod with a timer so that she could photograph herself, standing naked in classic poses in front of a background of cream colored silk curtains. Her surroundings were relaxed and tasteful; books, photographs, a few high end antiques mixed with modern furniture, black and white photos by Ansel Adams, Walker Evans, and Joel Peter Whitkin. She also had plenty of computer equipment, lights, and cameras. A trust fund bohemian, she'd never had to support herself, at least not until her family's recent bankruptcy. Even before that, though, she always lived with extreme frugality, horrified at the idea of "chipping into the principle." But now, with the income all but dried up, what was left of the principal was all she had to live on.

Chapter 7

Harry Waldheim's Journal

Of what value is trust when a thief and con artist, as I am, and completely untrustworthy myself, expects something more (or at least something different) to be served back? I think now that it was not so much a breach of trust, (but there is honor among thieves, is there not?), as it was being played for a fool (which I am), as an unequal among criminals. A fool with his guard down; complacent for fuck's sake! But wait, my criminal acts were never discovered, making me certainly far from morally superior (perhaps a better crook though) and, dare I say, a self-righteous hypocrite. Did I merely stumble across the truth?

So: who's the better of we two emotional twins, raised by drunken, knuckle dragging cretins? And, did I actually stumble, or was I led by her – a superior adversary whose game was not to escape detection at all, but rather to taunt; sophisticated coquette that she is? Did I merely discover a door left open by her, my beloved Pandora? Cryptic warnings written in code on the insides of my eyelids: "He who enters never returns." Or, perhaps she was only a medium, a vessel, a messenger, a figment of my imagination, a fiction. I made her up. I invented her. After all, isn't this just a story about a couple of abused children, and about three lost souls thrust into the same tiny room?

Born innocent, or at least in some momentary innocence at the second of conception; corrupted during incubation, if god forbid, we were a hideous surprise, our mothers regretting an inebriated evening of indiscretion with a man lacking in all but the crudest of qualifications. We advance forward in incubation, abused and unwanted; then are born already destroyed, resented and unloved; criminals all.

Chapter 8

Try as he might, Harry Waldheim just couldn't get his brain balanced. It probably didn't help that he'd spent several years during his hippy days high on Sandoz, Ozley, Orange Sunshine, or some other variety of LSD, ludes, speed or who knows what else. He rarely came up for air. Years later, if acquaintances from that era by chance met him on the street, they'd say, "Hey man...I thought you were dead." Harry would think the same thing about them, and on their separate ways they'd go. And that would be that, as he really didn't care to associate with the past ever again. It had been a good twenty years since he'd been an angry, self-loathing, aimless rebel and most of those other people were more clueless than before, still living in the past, all nostalgic for the *good times*.

A few decades later in his new *straight* life, inexplicably, he'd been driven to make drawings or paint a picture or most recently, write a novel. There was really no clear explanation for this drive. He had never been an artist as a child nor had he shown any interest in self- expression. Back then, he'd really had nothing much to say about anything. Perhaps psychedelic drugs actually did open something up. No matter, he just did what he did. Fuck the world. Sometimes the work just poured out.

He never intended it to happen, but five thousand pages of notes and thirty reference books later, three hundred pages of a rough manuscript appeared. None of this was easy and it often put him in deeply depressed states of mind, as this particular work was very close to the bone. He often wondered why he was so driven and enthusiastic, actually high at times and satisfied with what he had accomplished, though he would never show what he was doing to anyone. Ever.

At other times, though, he actively considered hanging himself. Harry had his demise all planned out. He had the rope and had identified the pipe, which was part of the overhead fire-extinguishing sprinkler system in his bedroom. He tested it and knew that it would support his weight. His prescription to Ambien was always maintained in the event that he might need a fist full of pills to help him on his way. He's spent hours imagining the perfect plan: He would craft the perfect noose, fasten the rope to the overhead pipe, swallow as many pills as possible, and climb up on his bed. He'd pull the noose tightly around his neck, whereupon he'd pass out in an Ambien stupor. The noose would cut off blood flow to his brain and that would be the end of Harry Waldheim. Bloodless and simple.

The super in his building would probably find him after the stench of his rotting corpse filled the building with fumes. A few friends would be sad for a brief period of time. His clueless parents would not have the faculties to understand what happened, having never grown emotionally beyond the age of eight years old. His girlfriend would happily move on and find an actual meaningful relationship. And maybe he'd be reincarnated as Harry Waldheim again and have to go through the same childhood, same parents, same periods of self-destruction, same inexplicable obsessions with self-expression, same manic/depression, and hang himself once again. Maybe he's been doing this for an eternity. Nothing to be afraid of, like brushing your teeth or tying shoes. This was just how it was, how it is, how it always will be.

Those daydreams, memories and distractions would often fill an entire day for Harry, who could simply sit at his cluttered desk, elbow on surface, hand on his head, finger obsessively working an eyebrow. Staring at nothing. Spaced out.

That was until he decided to spy on his increasingly distant girlfriend, Lately, Georgia seemed especially cold and unloving, almost unavailable. She wouldn't return phone calls and often ignored him when they were actually together. Finally, her suspicious behavior led him to do something he vowed to never do to anyone, having grown up with nosy, prying parents who gave him no privacy. He began snooping and reading her emails.

He wondered if this was another dream as he clicked through dozens of love notes between Georgia and her new secret lover. Access could not have been easier, they shared the same password. It had never occurred to either of them in the early days of their relationship, with their matching   internet   accounts,   that   passwords   were anything more than a formality.

From: Richard Lipschitz lipshitz@optonline.net
To: Georgia Pendleton Georgia.Pendleton@gmail.com
Subject: We do!!! have so much fun

We have so much to enjoy together...what a great position yesterday afternoon. I promise not to jerk off- saving it for my new and favorite student.

RL-

From: Georgia Pendleton Georgia.Pendleton@gmail.com
To: Richard Lipschitz lipshitz@optonline.net
Subject: Yes

Let's do explore. I love new. I do care and want to take care of you as my pet, as you said, as my lover too. You need to show me things you know—I need and want that. You've started and I love it. We can be however we feel like outside the home: with you as my slave for instance. I'm glad you want to try that. The more adventure the better. I have a lot to undo before I am free—adventure will help. You just have to help me unload Harry... Please, please be patient...

From: Richard Lipschitz lipshitz@optonline.net

To: Georgia **Pendleton** Georgia.Pendleton@gmail.com
Subject: xx

So nice to hear. I am comfortable with you but I have a long way to go. Thank you for sharing what's going on in your life with me. The last few weeks have been so great for me. I can only hope that you have enjoyed them as much as me. Let's keep going and see where life takes us.

From: Georgia Pendleton Georgia.Pendleton@gmail.com
To: Richard Lipschitz lipshitz@optonline.net
Subject: Us

I really like you. You are sexy. I have had a great time with you. It's been fun, you make me laugh.

From: Richard Lipschitz lipshitz@optonline.net
To: Georgia Pendleton Georgia.Pendleton@gmail.com
Subject: Love

Love is a state of mind. When I got your v-mail I could not get into your arms fast enough. I love to see U smile.

From: Richard Lipschitz lipshitz@optonline.net
To: Georgia Pendleton Georgia.Pendleton@gmail.com
Subject: Re: Love

Hi baby!! What a wonderful day I had yesterday. Woke up thinking of you. I own you- feel it more now. Fell asleep dreaming of you in my arms.

From: Georgia Pendleton Georgia.Pendleton@gmail.com

To: Richard Lipschitz lipshitz@optonline.net
Subject: First trip

I look forward to all of our dates.

How are your nipples? I want them!

And your balls. I want them too!!
All of you!!!!!

From: Georgia Pendleton Georgia.Pendleton@gmail.com
To: Richard Lipschitz lipshitz@optonline.net
Subject: First trip

It's 2.5 hours to Newport. I looked at a lot of inns and booked one. I think of you when I wake up and you must be in my dreams. Can't wait for our first trip together.

PS: Harry returns tonight...yuck!!!

xxx-G

Harry found himself overwhelmed by sadness and self-pity. He felt completely alone, betrayed and abandoned. It seemed he was continuing a life-long pattern of over forty, often painful, years of parental abuse, bullying, and myriad girlfriends almost as complicated as he. Paralyzed by melancholy, he reread this last sentence, *Harry returns tonight, yuck!* The throbbing in his head strengthened as he slid from his chair to the hard wooden floor and curled up into a fetal position, his brain fleeing elsewhere. He was falling through a pulsing black hole, a sky diver, arms and legs wide open, flying through a dark void.

Chapter 9

Harry Waldheim's Journal

It's not all that common when stars line up and the universe is in harmony, paving the way for a perfect collision. What are the odds that three tiny specs of insignificant matter could ever even come in contact, let alone combine to create a new life form? But that is what's happening. Is it a quantum leap or just a stellar aberration? But what do I know about anything, acting only on instincts, as did my guardians and those before them. My world will certainly never be the same. This is my informal education... in its finest hour. Search no more you fool; study these lessons and read the fine print.

Chapter 10

The morning after Harry's suspicions were aroused, he crawled out of bed, still groggy and fogged by Ambien. Lying was nothing new for Georgia, but what was this about? At least he got to sleep— well, more like knocked out and blasted—a dreamless coma; but it was something like sleep. He thought about Georgia. Was she actually ever really his girlfriend? More likely his girl-situation, he scoffed to himself. No matter.

"Who's fucking with me?" he wondered out loud. "Guess I'll give ole Becky Johnson a call."

"Becky. Hey..."

"What?" she grumbled. She sounded more than a little hung over and not too happy about being awake.

"How about those Giants?" asked Harry, feigning enthusiasm.

"What the fuck? Who is this?"

"Ahhh...it's Harry Waldheim, Georgia's friend."

"What the hell'r you talking about?"

"Football."

"I hate football!"

"Really, you hate football? Well, the games are quite exciting in real life, actually."

Becky had no idea what he was talking about. "How about we just hang up NOW!"

"Don't get upset Beck. I was just calling to say I had a great time at your party a few months ago...lots of interesting people."

She slammed down the landline next to her bed.

"Okay...talk later then." Harry knew she was no longer on the line.

Well, that was the precise answer he was looking for. Georgia was lying, yet again. Who was she with? As adrenaline coursed through his veins, Harry's focus was clear. His suspicions were correct, his instincts, sharper than ever. He felt as though he could see through walls, walk on water, shape shift and time travel.

"This is good," he said out loud. He could return to that familiar place, the source of his strength and genius: pain.

Harry's brain was firing on all twelve cylinders, like a souped-up monster truck, as two grime encrusted ruffians began ripping up the street five stories below with an obnoxious cacophony of staccato jackhammer bursts. All this was in addition to deep blasts from the aggressive, compound horn of a fire truck, the siren of which, echoed through canyons of cement, brick, and steel. The heroes in the red truck self-righteously shoving all living things aside, mostly for sport and to wage their version of class warfare on anyone not wearing their uniform.

"Where's the fucking fire, assholes?" Harry shouted into the street beneath him.

A changed Harry stared out the window; he no longer felt sorry for himself. Like an amateur boxer, he needed to take a few punches to awaken his primal anger. He needed to see his own blood. Like the time as a 10 year old, Richard Leesome, twice his size, bloodied Harry's nose. He dove for the bigger kid's throat knocking him to the ground, covering the bully's face with blood and snot. Harry could go berserk when angered. A victim no longer, altered and distorted, he was beginning to focus, like dynamite on a laser beam.

"Bring it on," he fumed aloud, as the sky exploded, suddenly dumping rain and a blitzkrieg of flashing lightning. In his head, he heard the loud music of Glen Branca's Fourth Movement; a comet on a collision course was heading toward Manhattan.

Chapter 11

The next day

Resembling a pink, greased pig, drenched in his own slime and sweat, Richard Lipschitz removed the ball gag from his willing mouth, skillfully unbuckling the strap with one hand while he rolled over on his back. He had just been reamed by his most recent, eager and beloved *student*, Georgia Pendleton. Gushing and high from all this, he couldn't have been more pleased that the two of them had so quickly become addicted to their daily afternoon *lessons*. They had gone much better than he could have imagined.

Richard mostly just wanted to get fucked and played with and pleasured while he passively and submissively accepted the attention. He *topped from the bottom*. And the sessions improved every day with new toys and devices and positions. With the enthusiastic Georgia he had struck gold. There was nothing she wouldn't try or do.

"Hand me my panties, and please baby, turn down the music," Georgia said. The Tony Bennett CD, one of Richard's favorites, continued to blast until she reached over and turned it down herself. She sat up, grabbed a cigarette without lighting it, and put her knees up. She appeared spent and worried. She looked around the bed for her underwear and then turned her eye to Lipschitz. He had managed to put them on, under the covers, another of his clever skills. "Now that's the way it should be," she purred, every bit the eager little sex kitten.

"I think you're ready," he chuckled. "You should sign up for Chunxx's *semen-ar*." He was a self-professed master of non-sequiturs and bad puns. This one caused his more than ample diaphragm to convulse with laughter—silly and smashed and so very proud and happy that he had made it all the way to Park Avenue and was now banging a rich trophy WASP.

"Yeah...C-H-U-N-X-X," he spelled. "She got that name as a kid, teased for being overweight. So she was like, okay, fuck you, I'm Chunxx in your face and up your ass, bitch! And that was that. Now she's the best dominatrix in town."

"What? Chunxx? Who's Chunxx? Tell me more."

"She's also my best friend, my BFF...whatever... I want you two to meet 'cause she's a great lady, a teacher. I've told her all about you...and us." He fished a dog-eared business card from his beat-up wallet, a chaotic mess of wadded-up ones, scratched family snapshots and Duane Reade receipts. "Here," he handed Georgia the card, "drop her a line ASAP. I know for a fact she'd love to meet you."

Richard Lipschitz described himself as a family man, a man invested in his community, a man with a great sense of humor, an ethical man, a devout Jew. A self-defined submissive, he was training Georgia to be his dominant, or rather, the dominant he wanted: one who would do exactly what he wanted, when he wanted it. In actuality, they often just improvised variations on sexual themes. They had been fucking almost every afternoon since the night they met at Becky Jackson's party.

Chapter 12

"I can't fucking find anything in this fucking dump," Harry screamed aloud, after losing his reading glasses for the third time in the same day. He scanned eclectic stacks of books, vinyl records, CD's, reel-to-reel audio tapes, players and decks, speakers, amplifiers, guitars synthesizers, photographs, magazines, plants and a few buried sticks of furniture. His once large and open loft was overflowing with gear and toys affording only a few paths leading from couch to kitchen to bathroom to bedroom. Urban neurosis from years of distractions had made him a frenetic bundle of nerves—an unfocussed dabbler going in too many directions.

A well-hidden gun safe, buried in the back of a closet behind stacks of shoes and a rack of abandoned business suites in garment bags was now all but forgotten. Installed with great care and cunning, his inherited collection of World War Two rifles, pistols, daggers, a bayonet and two defused German hand grenades, sat in the locked case which had not been opened since the early days, when Harry first moved in. Back in the days when living and working in the same place was the thing to do.

In the past, he paid his bills working efficiently, as he would say...but actually working as little as possible. He produced television commercials while dismissing the corporate world as worthless, vapid and hateful. Now, as luck would have it, he'd come into an inheritance. The recent death of a long lost uncle—an eccentric, fascist, loner from Bavaria—set

Harry up for life, leaving him with sufficient funds to live in modest comfort. And so, for Harry, at least one distraction was out of the way: having
to make a living.

Georgia was in the shower with the bathroom door wide open. Steam
billowed out into the room as she methodically scrubbed every inch of
her tight body. A five foot three former gymnast, her muscle tone defied
her 42 years.

An exhibitionist and a tease, once out of the shower, she walked
around the loft, naked, pretending to ignore Harry. He loaded the evening's footage into his computer, pretending to ignore her, in turn, as the
sounds of Moby filled the air. On the computer screen, an overhead view
revealed Georgia and Harry joined at the pelvis. The video was solarized,
the filtered colors almost psychedelic, the slowed-down motion very
dream-like. The audio was distorted to a lower frequency and made her
clanging bracelets sound like heavy elephant chains. Harry lingered a moment, watching, and then, changing modes, meandered toward the
kitchen.

"I'm considering plastic surgery," Georgia said, as she toyed with the
pasta salad in a take-out container. Candlelight illuminated her tired
face.

Harry sat and ate while he listened with feigned interest to this latest
iteration of Georgia's mantra of nine years—the meditation on her fail-
ures and low self-esteem.

"Okaaay," he lied.

"No, I mean it. I've been thinking about it lately, and..."

Agitated and exhausted from nine years of this, he just couldn't do it
anymore. "You know, you have had way too much money. I mean, your
parents gave you way too much. Have you ever thought that's why you're
so friggin' bored? You're mixing up what's important with crap. What
are you doing? Why would you want to cut yourself up? Isn't that a form
of self-mutilation? Why don't you just concentrate on being a photographer. You're good at that. Develop it. Be obsessed with *it*, not your face!"

"Yeah... well... whatever."

Georgia frowned and drifted off into her own thoughts as Harry's words faded into the distance. *The only one who cares about my photography is pathetic Harry. How can that judgmental dick think he knows what's best for me? I just want to have fun with my new sexy boy-toy.* She imagined tying a ribbon around Richard's cock and nutsack, both of them giggling as he lay on his back, wearing lipstick and a woman's blouse, his wrists tied together with clear plastic wrap. She cradled his genitals like a baby bird; talking to them as though they could hear and understand her words of encouragement.

"Hey little fellas," she cooed, cupping the shaved, pink scrotum delicately in both hands, "Mommy's here to take care of you." She kissed and licked them, tenderly. Then she looked up slightly, inhaling, "Am I ignoring you, big guy?" She addressed Dick Lipschitz's limp pecker. "Why are you so small today?" She wrapped her thumb and forefinger tightly around the base, squeezing and cutting off the blood flow, as "little Dickie" began to slowly expand and lengthen, listing a bit to one side like a stunned, pink trout. If it had actually been a living fish, it only could have swum around and around, dumbly, in circles...

Chapter 13

Harry Waldheim's Journal

I have taken the bait...

Is birth a time for celebration or mourning? Has something new been created, or has some atomic structure simply been rearranged? Is energy neither created nor destroyed? And what about entropy, and a transition of chaos to some measure of order? In this case, three separate and disparate entities colliding and all hell breaking lose? What the cluster-fuck is being created here? I swallowed the bait— hook, line and sinker. I've signed up. I've consented. I've checked all the boxes. I'm in this for the duration. Finally I have something to live for, and I feel more alive now than I've felt for a very long time.

Chapter 14

Thoughts of the grunts of at least a dozen overgrown, corn-fed, steroid-enhanced, supersized stuffed kielbasas in spandex, the slamming and crunching; brick walls being demolished by wrecking balls; hitting a 12 point buck with a pick-up truck, cracking bone sounds like bags of brittle plastic being crushed by a steam roller echoed in Harry's fogged brain as a whistle signaled stop, and then the slamming repeated, over and over. What was this game about he wondered? In the extreme high definition close-ups, flesh and spandex looked like rubber. This is all fake. It can't really be happening, Harry mused, as the throbbing in his head increased.

"Helloo...." called Liv, across the table from Harry, "I didn't know you were such a football fan."

She'd ordered eggs Benedict. Harry had coffee, toast and scrambled eggs. He hadn't touched any of it. Harry was glued to the tube, ignoring his best friend, along with the host of art world trendies crammed into the place, having brunch, talking over one another. The only ones watching the Giants game seemed to be Harry and the bartender, a grey ponytailed Johnny Cash, all in black, who mechanically mixed Bloody Marys.

Coming to for a second, Harry winced. "Oh, sorry, I actually hate football. Always have. Now I hate it even more. I think something's up with Georgia."

"Why?" Liv frowned, scrunching her nose.

"I just know it. Something's not quite right."

They hadn't seen each other in a few weeks, yet were next door neighbors and extremely close friends. Liv was mainly obsessed with her painting and Harry with himself. True soul mates, their love was without condition. They even had sex once, but as comfortable and hot as it was they decided that their friendship was too important to ruin with sex and romance and all those capricious emotions associated with intimacy.

Liv tried to change the subject, since Harry looked so sad and obsessed. She knew her friend. She'd never seen him so dark and shut down. Trying to get his mind off whatever was eating at him, she said, "Check it out." She pushed her phone across the table to him. "It's the latest."

He glanced at the painting half-heartedly. "Nice, is it new?"

"Yeah, I painted it all in one day. It sort of painted itself."

"I like it," he offered, not actually looking. He was still glued to the T.V. The gladiators in spandex continued their endless grunting and crunching. *Coarse, rude, savage barbarians*, thought Harry.

The waiter slid them the check. Harry looked up, for a few seconds distracted from his dark world, eyed the waiter. *Looks like Justin Bieber with his perfectly quaffed hair, and those fucking skinny black jeans; fame high school grad no doubt.* Everyone in the restaurant had a similar look, all in black, all too cool for each other, looking about the same, except for the bartender, the older dude, watching the Giants game with one eye and mixing drinks with the other.

Outside, there was a chill of fall in the air. The sun was a bit lower in the sky. Liv and Harry walked on in silence until, finally, she relented and looked up at him. "Okay, tell me about it. What are your suspicions, Columbo?" Usually, a much shorter Liv had to trot to keep up with Harry. This time he'd slowed to such a crawl, she was practically dragging him down the sidewalk.

Harry turned to her. "Okay, look... She's, well, acting really weird. And she went to a Giants football game, at least I think she did. Who knows where she went, and with whom. She hates football!" Coming to a full halt, Harry stared blankly at the sidewalk as the memory began to take shape.

In high school, the entire football team hazed and harassed him, making his life more miserable than even his abusive parents could. He kissed Lynne

Wordsdorf in the back of a dark school bus returning from ski practice—he remembered her soft pale skin and blond hair smelled mildly of Dial soap and 16-year-old girl sweat. The down on the nape her neck was moist with his saliva. He sucked on a firm tasty earlobe and then gently bit. She remained seated, passively looking forward, pretending not to notice and then she turned her head to face him and pulled their young mouths together—lips to lips, virgin tongues thrusting in and out of mouths with the life force of fighting cocks. He slowly moved his hands downward. "That tickles," she said, breaking the spell. He looked away, wondering if his engorged pecker would ever find a home. He remembered taking a deep breath sadly resigned that he was still chaste, and likely to remain so. They never spoke again. She told her boyfriend, Jeff Buck, captain of the varsity football team and then word went out: "Kill Harry Waldheim!"

"Where were you?" Liv gently nudged him.

He turned toward Liv and managed to get back on track. "Sorry, I was just...whatever." He paused. "She's lying about something, for some reason, and I have to find out what it is."

"What are you going to ask?"

"Not sure."

Silently, they walked toward the movie theater marquee. *In Cold Blood* was playing.

What irony, thought Harry. *Fuck my fucking brain!*

"You're paranoid." Liv said

"That's right...I'm paranoid."

Chapter 15

Harry Waldheim's Journal

You know what's weird? Being with someone, I mean, in what you thought was a so-called meaningful relationship, who never really even liked you. "It was just a seven year layover," according to her emails with Roz Flemberg. Do you have any idea how easy it was to find out what you were up to? We had the same friggin' PASSWORD! I never even considered spying on you until now!

Early on in their relationship they got new email accounts together and simply decided that it would be fun to have the same password, out of trust—like blood brothers. Why would we ever distrust each other, Harry remembered thinking.

Chapter 16

From: Roz Flemberg r.flemberg@gmail.com
    To: Georgia Pendleton Georgia.Pendleton@gmail.com
    Subject: Leave that sick man now

People like Harry and your parents are holding you back. Harry is sick-sick-sick... He was only a stepping stone while you treaded water in the big city. (Your words.) No guilt; that's life. Screw him and your parents. Leave him and leave town ASAP!!

    Your loving Jewish stepmother, Roz

From: Georgia Pendleton Georgia.Pendleton@gmail.com
To: Roz Flemberg r.flemberg@gmail.com
Subject: Good advice

Harry is a problem and I don't know what to do about him. I do get it—he is sick, at least as sick as I am. You know me better than anyone!! Thanks for the advice.

Love, Gerogia

From: Georgia Pendleton Georgia.Pendleton@gmail.com
To: Richard Lipschitz lipshitz@optonline.net
Subject: We have so much fun

Going offline now. Hope you found the liner to your jacket so you stay warm. I'll be thinking of you. No donuts. No jerking off... Save it for me.

From: Georgia Pendleton Georgia.Pendleton@gmail.com
To: Richard Lipschitz lipshitz@optonline.net
Subject: You tomorrow

I want to see you tomorrow at 1011 Park. Call me. So happy you are back!

From: Georgia Pendleton teneleventeneleven@mac.com
To: Richard Lipschitz lipshitz@optonline.net
Subject: My new address

How do you like my new email address: teneleventeneleven. Now I can start my real career. Being your dominatrix has opened up a new world of possibilities for me. What do you think about calling me Maitresse Chanel? What a wonderful day I had yesterday. Woke up thinking of you. I own you—feeling it more and more now. Reading the new book you gave me, *The Loving Dominant*. Thinking of you and getting excited.

You are my pet. Harry returns from LA soon, would much rather be with you. Thanks for greeting me every morning—I really like that. I stopped taking my medication for two days; I get anxious and depressed so I'm starting again. I am so lucky to have you. I have a big black dildo waiting for you and I can't wait to strap it on.

Miss you, love, Georgia

From: Richard Lipschitz@optonline.net
To: Georgia Pendleton teneleventeneleven@mac.com
Subject: Re: You tomorrow

I am home alone surfing the web; we just spoke a few minutes ago. Get real...Harry is out of your life...stop the shit...it's just us now... accept the fact that we have found each other...everything else will fall into place. I want you to meet my dear friend Mistress Chunxx soon. You two will have a lot to talk about and she can teach you everything you need to know about how to make me happy and provide you with a new line of work. A month ago I would have been playing with myself and inserting the big black ding-dong, but now I have the lovely, formidable Maitresse Chanel!)

Regards, Richard Lipschitz [Gomez]

From: Georgia Pendleton teneleventeneleven@mac.com
To: Richard Lipschitz lipschitz@optonline.net
Subject: Maitresse Chanel

Dear Gomez—did not do profile yet
I'm 5'4"
110 lbs. soaking wet and waiting for your tongue need your help with profile

From: Richard Lipschitz lipschitz@optonline.net
To: Georgia Pendleton teneleventeneleven@mac.com
Subject: Donuts and stuff

No donuts and definitely not touching myself. The only way I could get hard today would be to see you again tonight.

Regards, Gomez

From: teneleventeneleven@mac.com
To: job-120917980@craigslist.org
Subject: $$$open-minded females needed for explicit photos - no faces used$$$

Have done this kind of work before and enjoyed it. Do you want only college age women? I am older with a very fit dancer's body and am very comfortable being nude. Will be happy to send pictures if you're interested.

Thank you-

From: Georgia Pendleton teneleventeneleven@mac.com
To: Richard Lipschitz lipschitz@optonline.net
Subject: I miss you

Today I am really tired [almost no sleep], but am going to the gym anyway and then having Harry come by to work on my photo studio set up and help him with some digital stuff of his. We'll have dinner here and then he'll leave early because I'll make him leave early. I'd much rather spend the day with you, believe me. I have to pay attention to Harry though and follow my instinct on when to get rid of him for good. In general we actually see very little of each other. Thinking of you...always
Georgia

From: elegantmaitresse.com
To: Georgia Pendleton teneleventeneleven@mac.com
Subject: Maitresse Chanel

Maitresse Chanel, you have received a new message from elegant-maitresse.com. You can now login to your new account. Don't forget to check out our chatrooms and discussion forums too!

The Elegant Maitresse team

Harry went online to check out the Elegant Maitresse website. He read what was offered in complete surprise and disbelief.

The first image looking something like the interior of a Chinese restaurant, featured red lacquered walls, fake marble columns, fake marble floor. A large wooden red X was fastened to one of the walls and covered with leather and chain restraints. It was called the Asian torture room and was serviced by an all Caucasian staff wearing long, straight-haired, jet black wigs and stuffed into skin tight black leather corsets and black leather micro-mini skirts.

Their collection of toys was not seen but listed:

Ball gag, ball and chain, bit gag, blindfolds, body harness, bondage belt, bondage body bags, wrist ankle and thigh bondage cuffs, bondage harness, leather and latex bondage hoods, leather and latex bondage mittens, bondage tape, boxing gloves, chains, clingfilm, crops, cross-dressing wardrobe, cock ring, collars, d-rings, adult diapers, dog cage, feathers, leather, rubber and metal floggers, funnel gag, gas mask, head harness, human pony gear, humbler, inflatable gag, leashes, long tail whips, monoglove, muzzle gag, nipple clamps, wood, leather and rubber paddles, leather and rubber posture collar, ring gag, rope, steel shackles, sleepsacks, spreader bar, straightjackets, ankle suspension cuffs, tens unit, violet wand, vacuum beds, weights, whips, wrestling mats...and much more..

Most of the activities, Harry had never heard of. Animal play, B&D, bastinado, birching, black snake, blood sports, bondage, branding, bottom, brown showers, canes, cock and ball torture, collared, decorative binding, discipline, encasement, fetish, flogger, golden showers, pony play, scat, scrotal expansion, sensory deprivation, slave, strapple, suspension, urtication, vanilla, wrapping, Wartenberg wheel, mindfuck.

His head exploded. The image of a cold blue steel .44 magnum barrel pressed to his forehead refused to go away—not that he wanted it to. He wondered, if he were to pull the trigger in his fantasy, would everything that he just found out go away? This somehow gave him hope...made him feel like he might have some kind of control over his life...and death.

Of course he couldn't stop then. He had to go and Google this Richard Lipschitz character. He found house, family, job, friends, and lots of pictures of the Lipschitz kids, skiing, swimming winning participation awards for who knew what and who cared. Then he began scouring Georgia's emails. There were pictures of Georgia and Lipschitz on the beach in Newport, bundled up in sweaters, smiling for the world to see how happy two people could be. He wondered if those were real smiles? Surely she was faking it—or brainwashed. Maybe she'd been drugged...certainly not smitten; no way could she have actually been having a good time...happy...no way! He discovered dozens of photographs exchanged during the course of this affair.

Devastated, stricken with terror and anxiety, he read and reread every email, hunting for information about Lipschitz; finding out where he lived, who he worked for, his wife's and children's names, and more photographs. Thus began his research and his new life, as his thoughts turned to revenge.

Harry remained at his computer until sunrise, oblivious to the sounds of the drunks on the street, five stories below, slurring insults at each other, with no apparent concept of the time. In hacker mode, he hardly even registered any of his surroundings, as his printer spat out dozens of hard copies of emails and photographs: Georgia and Lipschitz embracing on the beach, a selfie of the two of them nude on a motel bed, Lipschitz in the driver's seat mugging for the camera, mouth wide open, tongue down to his chin, and on and on.

After an entire night of research, he stumbled upon a Lipschitz personal ad on craigslist but as he clicked on it, another email popped up. It was four in the morning and Lipschitz was still at it. Well, so was Harry. Maybe we are more alike than not, he thought. There were four photographs, two shots of a ruler next to his six and a quarter inch erect penis, listing a tad to the right. The remaining two were selfies in a mirror, his face barely hidden behind a small camera. He just sent these to Georgia. What, was he looking for... her approval?

Harry turned his attention back to the craigslist ad:
Park Avenue guy seeking fun, masculine bottom for safe play
Reply to: personals-604460974@craigslist.org

44yo top guy, Park Avenue, 5'7", brn/blu, 165#, 7c, clean cut, masculine guy. Love making out, kissing, very oral, mutual sucking, long slow deep safe fucking. Looking for similar bottom guy 30s/40s. Please have pics, including a face shot.

"This is Georgia's new boyfriend?" Harry screamed. Exhausted, he rested on his back, like a zombie, in his dark apartment, the only illumination a crazy cartoon on television. The audio was turned off and the sounds of the city waking up seemed to be his only comfort as he stared, traumatized, at the ceiling. Finally, he passed out in a haze of a three-Ambien-induced dreamless, thoughtless, mind-numbing sleep.

Chapter 17

Harry Waldheim's Journal

Big fake smile vulgar oversized capped bleached teeth close cropped fake shoe polish black hair spray tan black tux bow tie posing delusional loser new couple big fake smiles posing

Dickhead roped tied strangled ball sack bound gagged tied wrists daughter's blouse flowered thin straps dark body hair cock baby bird naked ankles tied stupid smile bottom controls top...Tight stomach bound black cord trimmed pubis tight ass hand sized black thigh high vinyl boots spike heels posing whip hand tight fake breasts gold ribbon bound rope neck blonde dynell real estate lady hair Nazi officer cap face tired frown. Open legs sit anger pussy shaved lips exposed calves liver cunt black vinyl frame dark cord wrap fake breasts deformed nipples dog collar same Dynell real estate lady hair bitter frown Nazi cap.

Chapter 18

Driving the leased silver Lexus SUV, season tickets on the dashboard, Dick Lipschitz (he preferred Richard) took a healthy swig from the pocket-sized flask filled specially for the ride. The beer would begin to flow soon enough during the game, but for the drive it was straight vodka. He passed the flask over to Georgia, in the passenger seat. She threw down three strong gulps and then passed the remainder to the back seat, where Dick's half-brother Frank sprawled, barely awake. He waved her back and rolled onto to his side, still hung over from the past night's bender. The Lexus sped toward Giants Stadium deep in the heart of the New Jersey Meadowlands: a polluted swamp, a mafia body dump—the perfect place to play football.

Georgia looked over at Richard, gave him a slightly hairy eyeball, and unbuckled her seatbelt. She slid closer while Richard concentrated on the speeding traffic heading west on I-95. With her left hand she gave his thigh a teasing caress, while with her right hand she expertly unbuckled his belt and unfastened the button on his pants. His large gut tumbled out like a hanged man. She slid the zipper ever so smoothly down its length, kneading the ample folds of his sagging shaved belly and then moved in, snuggling her head under the steering wheel. She fished his cock out, hard as a tiny, warped Louisville Slugger and went down on him. Listing somewhat to the right, it looked like a dead, stiff, pink, brook trout bent to one side, rigid with rigor mortis. His cock glistened and shined with her saliva. She licked its purple head and stuck the pointy tip of her tongue into its tiny vertical smile, then removed it from her mouth. She looked warmly at her captive and rubbed it over her face, smelling its musk. She licked around the corona with her left fist firmly clamped on the shaft; it was harder than a rock, dorsal vein bulging. She continued to constrict the blood flow, providing an expert tourniquet with her thumb and forefinger as she squeezed the freshly-shaved base. She opened her mouth and throat wide and, like an anaconda deep throating a living rat, took the entire six-and-one-quarter inch hog down her throat, channeling Linda Lovelace. Her head bobbed up and down for a full ten minutes...until... Lipschitz, his vision blurred, blasted a hot gob of semen against the back of her throat and released an involuntary groan as they sped on toward the stadium.

Georgia sat, once again, in the passenger seat with her seatbelt on. She stared absently out the window, mesmerized by the endless swamp grasses of the meadowlands whizzing by. She tossed back the remainder of the vodka and still the unmistakable taste of cum lingered. She was completely oblivious to Lipschitz as he lip-synced to Springsteen. They pulled into the stadium parking lot that was already beginning to fill with a spectacle of SUVs, obesity, and garish displays of New York Giants nationalism. This was Georgia's first football game.

Still smashed after that half liter of vodka, but holding her own, Georgia emerged from the crowded ladies room. She met up with the Lipschitz brothers as they clowned their way out of the men's room after having each taken a long inebriated piss. They wore twin Giants fan outfits: triple-x red, white and blue jerseys along with silly little colored caps with Giants logos repeating around their perimeters. Georgia clicked several snapshots as they laughed drunkenly at their own foolish antics. They swilled super-sized cups of beer and made loud, groaning Giants fan noises while they posed for Georgia.

Lippy, (one of Dick's many nicknames) with his mouth wide open, tongue down to his chin in full cunnilingus mode, stole the show. She took more photos as he posed and mugged, with his tell-tale, hard drinker's, beet red facial capillaries. They chugged the last swallows from the super-sized plastic beer cups and headed to their seats, Georgia in tow, clicking snapshots on the way. Too smashed to have a thought in her head about the past or the future, she was oddly present and living in the moment. Not being judged or judging, she shuffled along—inebriated and happy. Looking down to the field, she mumbled "They look like gladiators," to no one in particular.

Chapter 19

At 1011 Park Avenue, on the 34th floor, Georgia was in the midst
of a project. She stood, coffee in one hand and a piece of a photograph in the other. Using the pictures she'd taken of herself
naked, she had cut them up with scissors: arms, breasts, legs, ass, facial
parts, vulva and cunt, and was in the process of reassembling the parts in
symmetrically patterned collages into a specially bound scrap book. Harry
sat on the couch, reading and keeping her company.

He now knew what was going on, having neurotically read and reread
all the emails. He spent four hours that morning, trying to run off his
anxiety, burning as much cortisol as possible. The Klonopin was kicking
in and he was finally calm.

She assembled her portfolio and then inadvertently knocked it off the
table. The book split apart and photos scattered everywhere.

"Fuck!"

"What?" Harry asked with fake concern, enjoying her agitation.

Georgia quickly picked up the mess on the floor and examined her
aging face in the mirror. "This is frustrating, putting this fucking thing
together."

"Maybe you need a better bookbinder," suggested Harry, toying with
her frustration. Knowing that she didn't know that he knew gave him an
illusion of control over the situation.

She ignored him and remained preoccupied with her image in the mirror. Despising what she saw, with no control over her mortality—an ancient hag, unloved, misunderstood and disrespected, she took a swig of vodka, which she thought she had so cleverly disguised as plain water. She slid a bright red lipstick across her thin, wrinkled, upper lip, then pressed it to the lower and stood back, with a hopeful look. Exasperated, she slammed the lipstick to the floor. "Wrong fucking color. Shit!"

"Now what?" inquired Harry, faking calm concern, "Need some new lip shit?" Momentarily amused, and very pleased with his pun.

But then it hit him.

Time slowed.

He was a fool.

A fool who just gave away his secret, and his only power over a situation that if he'd just kept his mouth shut he might have been in control of, forever.

Why so premature? If he was truly a con man and a criminal, he would have stayed quiet and played them both for a good long while. He could've spied on them, hovering like god, quietly watching their lives unravel, witnessing their fights. He might have come to her rescue, a hero in her weakest moments of low self-esteem and abandonment. Maybe he could've won her back, or at least taken her away from *him*. Lipschitz was, after all, married with three kids. What could he actually provide for Georgia?

Poor Harry just couldn't keep his mouth shut. He had to say lip shit. In the end, his desire for her to know that he knew proved more powerful than any need to bat the two of them around like a cat with a couple of mice.

Georgia's only response was silence.

Now she knew.

Their lives would never be the same after this. Neither of them spoke. She remained at the mirror, her back turned to him, watching him in the reflection.

Harry got up to leave.

"Good bye," he lied.

From: Richard Lipschitz lipschitz@optonline.net
To: Georgia Pendleton g.nabokov@gmail.com
Subject: Candlewood Lake

Only if it works out, we can go ice skating, then a movie, then more crazy sex at Park Avenue. I will help you relax and you will help me.

Gomez

From: Georgia Pendleton g.nabokov@gmail.com
To: Richard Lipschitz lipschitz@optonline.net
Subject: Candlewood Lake

That's so sweet, we will have a great time together
     Love, G

From: Richard Lipschitz lipschitz@optonline.net
To: Georgia Pendleton g.nabokov@gmail.com
Subject: travel plans

Let's make travel plans as soon as we can. I can slip away from the family any time. They'll just think it's business. Tell Harry you need some space and just want to be alone and if he calls don't answer. He should eventually get the idea that you are finished with him. You are a nice person...let's make plans later tonight. Call when you can after 9:30. The forecast is 30% chance of rain and 100% chance of happiness for us!!

     XOXOXO Gomez

Chapter 20

Harry Waldheim's Journal

Her carefully constructed web of lies is a source of pride and accomplishment; a sculpture; a work of art; something bigger than life; a concoction from nothing. Is truth a great destructive force – splitting her world into tiny bits? "How dare you disrespect my fine work and ruin it." Her lies are her creation, her expression, her essence, her religion, her soul....her truth.

Chapter 21

Number one Knoll and Gorge Drive: phone message: "Hello, it's the Lipschitz residence. Please leave a message and someone will get right back to you. Have a great day!" The affable man's voice on the answering machine is none other than that of Richard Lipschitz. It took him twenty attempts and over two hours to create the message, but he finally got it perfect.

"Still no answer," Harry muttered to himself as he skulked away from yet another payphone. They were hard to find in Manhattan so he managed to put in quite a few miles thinking he'd be covering his tracks if all his calls were from different phones, in case they were traceable. He didn't want to leave a message, preferring to hear the actual voice of Richard Lipschitz, but who knew how Harry would respond, his mind racing at the speed of light.

It was Monday morning, the day after the Giants game. Richard was extremely hung over. In a dense fog, he looked into the mirror of the small bathroom connected to the guest room where he slept now, almost every night (except on the occasions when he passed out in the man cave he built years ago, in the basement). His image slipped in and out of focus as he stared at himself in the mirror. He applied a final dab of glue to his bald skull and fussily attached his hairpiece and straightened his necktie. With unwarranted vanity, he gazed at his blurred reflection and produced a giant fake smile, revealing super-white, oversized capped teeth. Pushing his lips out of the way to reveal pink gums, he scrubbed them with a stumpy forefinger. His second double chin moved into place as he opened wide, stuck his tongue out, and attacked it with a u-shaped metal scraper to remove the yellow scum.

After a slow, dense, contemplative morning crap of alcoholic asphalt, he repositioned himself in front of the mirror, ignoring the chaotic noise of his family preparing for their day.

Sarah, his wife of sixteen years, was in the kitchen getting their children ready for school. All three were in special education, with varying degrees of ADHD, dyslexia, and child obesity. In short, clones of their parents.

The children bickered in loud voices. "Mom, can I get another bagel?" one yelled.

"No!" Sarah shouted in response as she packed their lunches.

"You just had one," yelled the youngest.

"Yeah, so can I have another one?"

"You're fat."

"Shut up you guys, you're both fat!"

The kids all laughed and high-fived.

"Here guys, some more bacon." Like a short order cook, Sarah slid another plate filled with bacon in front of the hungry youngsters.

The eldest Lipschitz child smiled, got up, and put another bagel in the toaster.

"Me too!" demanded Richard junior. "I'm hanging out with Will tonight. We're studying for a social studies test. I hate that class."

"You're so gay!" screamed the other two siblings in unison.

His daily hour of primping almost over, Dick re-straightened his pale yellow necktie. He tried out another big, fake, super-white, capped-toothed smile, before performing a final check of his glued-on hair.

"Looking good." He wolf whistled.

Impeccably dressed for business, he made his way through the hallways of the cluttered, split-level suburban house, past mangled cardboard boxes and torn garbage bags spewing a family history of old plastic toys, comic books and half-stuffed, stuffed animals. Speeding through the kitchen, he shoved a doughnut into his pumpkin face, and swilled a second cup of coffee. He paused long enough to kiss all the kids on the tops of their heads and scratch under the chin of Jack, their yellow labradoodle. Faking hot attraction, he groped his wife's giant ass. "Love you Sarah...got some meetings tonight. I'll be late," then exaggerating his Bronx accent he added, "I gotta netwoik....gotta bring home da bacon."

"Yeah?" she replied, not believing one word. "Good, because the kids can't seem to get enough," Sarah chuckled sarcastically.

Richard Lipschitz thought of himself as an upstanding family man, a good neighbor. In fact, he didn't actually know his neighbors. The Lip-schitz house was the only one in the neighborhood that hadn't been torn down and replaced by a McMansion. He was active in his synagogue, mostly as a place to schmooze, where he attempted to cast his net in search of more business opportunities. Nothing ever came of it because his fellow congregants saw him as superficial and no one took him seri-ously. And his community, like his immediate family, mostly ignored him. In his mind, he was the center of the universe, the smartest man in the room; to the rest of the world, Richard Lipschitz was an irrelevant zero. He was clueless and completely oblivious.

If you were heading west on the Merritt Parkway, driving next to Dick Lipschitz, you would see a businessman, suit and yellow tie, in his shiny new silver Lexus SUV yakking on his mobile phone with one hand, the other pounding the steering wheel to the beat of something. If you were riding with Dick, you would hear Billy Joel singing, *It's my life*. Dick would be singing at the top of his lungs, completely out of tune, unless he was on the phone. If you only had the visual, you might think: now there's a typical tycoon—making deals, buying and selling, making split second decisions, a true captain of capitalism, a type A, multi-tasking while driving.

If you were sitting next to him, however, you would know that he was three months behind on the leased Lexus SUV. You would hear him whine, "Yes...can you make that by later today? Look, it has to be... Yes of course, but what matters is.... But can you get the transfer to go through and send it to Matt? Of course, naturally, I said I would! What? There's only forty dollars left in the account?!"

Richard Lipshitz was broke. And, he was fired. Sacked, yet again—an annual occurrence. He sold financial instruments, whatever that meant, and yet knew very little about the economy or finance or the stock mar-ket. In fact he could barely balance his own checkbook; that was his wife's job.

Lipschitz glanced at his reflection in the rearview mirror. "Making the m-o-n-e-y," he thought to his delusional self, mugging to the mirror. A 45-year-old pudgy master of the universe, he pulled into the parking lot of his soon-to-be-former work empire, a two story steel and glass corporate box in Greenwich, Connecticut. There were a total of twenty employees inside, amid five thousand square feet of computers and monitors. Workers were glued to their stations, crunching numbers. No one looked up. The only sounds were the clicking of fingers on keyboards and the Bloomberg Business Channel, barely audible, on several large flat screen monitors. This was the world of the hedge fund manager: bundling, buying and selling all manner of collateralized debt obligations, credit default swaps, convertible securities, derivatives, mortgage backed securities, and on and on, bean counting their way to billions.

Lipschitz, coffee in one hand, doughnut in the other, surveyed the activities of the twenty employees as he walked quickly through the office, slurping from his mug. All was in order, he pretended. The well-oiled machine was efficiently churning out pots of money at the speed of light. There was only one problem—he was there to pick up his final paycheck. He walked around like he owned the place, but, in reality, he'd been canned, downsized, sacked, fired, and he was completely ignored. Nobody actually understood what he did there anyway.

"Good day to you," Lipschitz chirped at the receptionist, still imagining himself as master of the universe. She cautiously looked up, said nothing, and handed him an envelope. Once that was done, she continued her work, not missing a beat. He said hello to a series of soon to be former team members as he walked through the vast, open office filled with mazes of quants, accountants, and various bean counters staring like robots at computer screens. No one acknowledged him as he left. In his arms, he cradled a cardboard box filled with Giants football and Yankees baseball souvenirs, memories of the events that were most important to him.

On his way out, the security guard opened the door and then closed it with a swift pull, blocking his return. He didn't look back because, really, he didn't care. This was his fourth sales job in four years. Ever the delusional optimist, he was back in the leased silver Lexus SUV, singing out to his reflection in the rearview mirror, "Who cares about the repo man. I'm heading down the highway to New York fuckin' cittay! For some meetings, BITCH!" He popped a Nigel Stern motivational CD into the deck:

Dudes, I headed out on my own the other night...went to a strip club and really got my mojo working. I talked to a bunch of strippers which really boosted my confidence before I went to my first club. I began talking to all these random women passing by on the sidewalk. Talking to those strippers somehow gave me strength and so I wasn't as intimidated by all the beautiful women I encountered that night. Some of them even seemed to like me. What a surprise! I even flirted with several hot girls. Only wish I got a number. I said hello to a few more girls and made some eye contact at another club, complimenting them on their great looks. I felt like a real sex machine even though I never hooked up...but still had a really great night!

Chapter 22

Georgia, already wearing a thick plastering of makeup, laid out an assemblage of black patent leather, thigh-high stilettos, a short red leather skirt, and a tight black corset. There was something slightly off about this outfit, she thought, but still, *this could be something.*

Georgia Pendleton was a child of apparent privilege: private schools, world travel, exclusive summer camps, sophisticated, cultured, rich WASP friends. Somewhere in her distant past, a vague connection to a Russian royal family—her father's mother's fifth cousin once removed, or something. She would often tell complete strangers at bars and parties that she was a Russian princess, after a few shots of vodka.

While she acted like she came from very old money, the truth of the matter was that she and her family were running out of cash. Her father had recently declared bankruptcy for the third time. Her mother, of some unverifiable background, seemed only capable of "employment" as a volunteer at the local public television station. Meanwhile, Georgia, always pretending to have unlimited funds, rarely paid her way when she went out with friends. "I just don't have any cash with me," she would declare, sometimes opening her empty wallet as proof.

At 1011 Park Avenue, Apartment 34L, as Richard Lipschitz neared the city for his "meetings," Georgia was in the process of getting all dolled up for the very same event. Feeling uncharacteristically hot, posing, she fantasized: *I'm going to learn the exotic arts of bondage, discipline, and sadomasochism. I'm going to become a dominatrix. I'm going to make Richard very happy, and make lots of money. Finally, a career.*

Standing naked in front of the full length mirror, she slid the fishnet stockings up each slender leg, then smoothly rolled the remainder just up to her freshly shaven pubis. She assumed a variety of provocative poses: prying apart her vulva while biting her lower lip, caressing her breasts, standing defiantly, arms folded, feet apart.

She had the body of a twelve-year-old girl with medium-sized fake breasts, and yet her face looked much older. At 43, she could pass for 63, and often applied gobs of makeup and fillers in an attempt to hide the wrinkles and fissures riddling her upper lip.

From Harry's perspective, she was perfect, with almost the body of a child. He was able to overlook Georgia's aging face. Nothing turned him on more than watching his cock plunge in and out of her cunt and asshole, tight and manicured, often with his camera in hand, zoomed in. And besides, she was planning on getting a facelift in the near future.

Sliding into the red leather micro-mini skirt, pulling up the thigh high black vinyl stilettos, and finally wrestling on the tight black leather corset, her outfit was complete. The effect was incongruous, unnatural, and she looked extremely uncomfortable and constricted. Even so, seeing her transition in the mirror gave Georgia a jolt of hope and optimism she hadn't felt for a very long time. She slipped on her beige Burberry trench coat, the one she'd had since prep school, and her bug-eyed Gucci sunglasses and headed downtown by taxi in her newly disguised identity.

The cab dropped Georgia off on 37th Street between 5th and 6th Avenues. It was a typical, late afternoon in the garment district: loud Puerto Ricans rolling racks of coats, dresses and blouses of all styles, colors, and sizes up and down the block, Orthodox Jews, in their long black wool coats and oversized black Stetson hats, hurrying to their next meetings, mindless of the other people, or traffic, on the street.

Georgia pulled out a scrap of paper with the address. Oddly, it turned out to be the freight entrance of a twelve-story garment manufacturing building. She checked it again and then handed the scrap of paper to the ancient, scruffy freight elevator operator, who eyed her knowingly and motioned for her to enter. He roughly slid the well-worn steel gate closed and manually cranked the lever, coaxing the elevator up. Georgia and the old man rode up to the eighth floor in silence, the air permeated with hints of electric motor ozone, axle grease, fabric sizing, and the body odor of the craggy, unwashed man working the lever. Only glancing at him for a moment, she registered his tobacco-stained teeth, his face buried like a pile of brush in a craggy, wrinkled face, covered in day-old-stubble, not to mention the unruly barbs of thick grey wires sprouting from his ears and nostrils and off the top of a bulbous, syphilitic nose. After an interminable amount of time, he cranked the control lever 90 degrees to the vertical position, bounced the elevator to a stop, and the ancient steel grate opened. It screeched, in desperate need of lubrication.

Georgia, not without trepidation, stepped out of the elevator and into her new world. She was greeted by none other than Mistress Chunxx. Although this was only their first meeting, Chunxx gushed, "I have heard so much about you! Welcome to your new home, Georgia," she fawned. Extending a slender right hand, pretending with all her might to appear confident and brave, Georgia greeted her new mentor. "The pleasure is all mine, Mistress," she intoned, squatting in an unnatural curtsy, as if meeting the Queen Mother.

"Have a look around and introduce yourself to the others. We'll be getting started in about ten minutes. But now I have at least a few hundred details to attend to. We have to shut the place down in a few weeks. The building will be converted to luxury condominiums this year. Can you imagine moving all this equipment out of here? And to where? Perfect! Anyway, that's not your problem. You're here to learn, and I've been told you are a very good and willing student, and I am personally looking forward to your training."

Mistress Chunxx spun to leave, pointing toward a few milling older doms, obvious pros, sporting well-worn corsets and thigh high stilettos. One of the older gals was wearing a slightly tattered Marlin Brando style black leather biker's cap. Well into their 40's and second gin and tonics, they chatted quietly among themselves, occasionally side-eyeing Georgia and the other obvious newbies, dressed in their shiny, virgin black vinyl and leather dominatrix outfits.

"Okay...places everyone!" ordered Chunxx. From the other room, she screamed at a hapless gimp wrapped in tight black leather and zippers. "Get the drinks ready...and...you worthless turd...get the new girl a glass of Perrier with two shots of vodka on the rocks! Now!"

A moment later, Georgia gratefully accepted the offering from the quivering, scrawny man. Later, she learned he was called Fido. He was a volunteer slave, there of his own accord. "Thank you for letting me serve you, mistress," he whined in an extremely effeminate subservient manner.

Was this guy for real wondered Georgia, as she threw down two Klonopin tablets, polishing off the remainder of the Perrier and vodka in the next gulp.

The gimp handed her a kind of brochure, a guide to the dungeon with a floor plan and descriptions of the various rooms available to clients. Georgia began to quietly look it over:

The Torture Chamber... as you crawl before your mistress, and your eyes focus upon the lantern lit chamber, you will realize that your fate has absolutely been sealed. Tremble as you behold so many instruments of pain: a spanking bench, an array of CBT (cock and ball torture) instruments, a bondage chair with adjustable legs, a foot worship throne, a nine-foot double sided rack with overhead bondage suspension system. Each piece has been hand carved by a master craftsman with painstaking attention to detail. The room also boasts a leather swing for strap-on play fantasies—and for the ultimate in bondage and four point suspension—a wooden restraint cage

She skimmed the next several pages: the Wrestling Room, the Sanctum, the School Room, the China Doll Room, the Medical Chamber, and on and on.

My new world, imagined Georgia. The Klonopin began its relaxing effect and her anxiety dissolved into calm. Ready to embrace all of these strange new people and images, she fantasized about the world of water sports, enemas, electric shock torture, leather restraints, and padded gurneys. She prepared to step out of her old, despised skin and climb aboard—accepted and exhilarated.

Georgia and four other novices were escorted into the Wrestling Room. The mistress welcomed them all, introducing herself, and then...Richard Lipschitz arrived. Dressed in his dark blue suit, crisp white shirt, pale yellow necktie, and shiny businessman shoes, his spray-on tan, fake capped white teeth, and glued on hair were all still in place. He stood at ease, relaxed, looking down toward the floor. Here, he appeared freed from the weight of his master of the universe persona. His demeanor conveyed that this was his true self, his calling, perhaps even his finest hour. "Shall we begin girls? Let's get to work," barked Mistress Chunxx.

Lipschitz gave Georgia a quick wink, which she secretly returned. He loosened his tie and began undressing, meticulously placing the articles of clothing on a chair. Two female novices helped him into a shiney, red, vinyl restraining suit covered with D-rings and leather belts, while two others strapped on a ball gag carefully tightening the head harness, and ordered him to his hands and knees on the grey padded platform. "We own you pissant, and we are going to punish you," the novices, joined by Georgia, read in unison from Chunxx's carefully typewritten script.

The suit left his cock and balls exposed, as well as his anus. His hard-on betrayed his otherwise relaxed demeanor. The two women forced a ridiculous, Dynel blonde wig over his own ridiculous hair piece. Lipschitz got down on all fours as the five novice dominatrices surrounded him, wearing their brand new strap on dildos.

Mistress Chunxx supervised and instructed them. "Okay, we're going to take turns performing anal intercourse on our volunteer. Two of our resident doms, Mistress Viona and Mistress Nikki will go first to show you the proper and safe way to perform this act. He's already given himself an enema, haven't we Lippy?"

He responded in the affirmative, "ummmm-hmmmm," the ball gag muting his voice, and nodded his head, obediently.

"Now, lubrication is of the utmost importance." Chunxx gouged out a wad of petroleum jelly from a gallon jar and spread it over Richard Lipschitz's eagerly awaiting butthole. "Next, we have to slowly stretch his sphincter to relax the muscles and not damage any tissue." She turned her attention to him. "Have we been doing our stretching exercises, Lippy?" she asked, teasingly. Again, he nodded in the affirmative. "Since I have very long fingernails and have an aversion to poop, I'm going to insert this small anal plug first. "Don't be afraid girls. Come in for a closer look, this asshole won't bite."

The girls giggled nervously and inched in. Chunxx handed Georgia a larger butt plug, which she slowly and carefully inserted.

"As you can see ladies, today's volunteer is quite stretched and ready for action. And now I'm going to let you girls go wild with your strap-ons. How does that sound?"

The five novices got to work, one at a time shoving their dildos into the ecstatic Lipschitz. Two of them spanked his face with their rubber cocks as Georgia, the last in line, prepared her dildo by rubbing an extra amount of lube on it. She shoved it in to the hilt and smacked his ass with a riding crop as she thrusted harder and harder. The others stood back, somewhat in awe of her performance.

"We have a very enthusiastic natural here," announced Chunxx, "Girls, take note, our new friend has talent!"

She turned back to the others, scolding, "Is that all you got for me ladies? Work that hole... This sissy boy is not afraid of pain. Drill this cunt to Chinatown.

They all took turns banging him again. Chunxx lit a cigarette and when they were done, flicked her ash on Lipschitz's head, then yanked out the ball gag. "Stick out your tongue, dipshit!" He obeyed immediately. Chunxx removed the cigarette from her collagen filled lips, spit a giant lougie in his mouth, and put the cigarette out on his tongue.

"How's that taste, sissy boy?"

"Ummmmmmm...aaaahhhhheeeee," he responded with a mix of pain and pleasure.

"Now stand the fuck up, pissant."

He stood, shaking all over...

"Now look up to the ceiling, cunt."

When he obeyed, Chunxx sucker punched him in the solar plexus with all her might. "Aaaaaaahhhhhhhhhhhuuuuurrrggggg!" He doubled over in pain, and then began to laugh with diabolical abandon.

Lipschitz gathered his belongings and limped away to the dressing room and Chunxx began her wrap-up. "Girls, that was truly an amazing first session. I'll expect you all back here next week, same time same place, for now. As you have probably heard, we'll be moving out of here in a month or so. If any of you have any thoughts about a new location for us, please feel free to speak up. Now get changed and we'll see you next week."

The dressing room looked very much like the locker room of any typical worn-out gym, having seen a lot of action over the past ten years. The steel doors were smudged and rusting from a little too much humidity and the air was thick with odors of patchouli, bergamot, sweet saccharin, rose water, Civet cat, ham, limburger cheese, tuna fish, pussy, used dildos, soiled costumes, moldy sneakers, and more, as though all of humanity had traveled through the place.

Once back in the lobby, Georgia turned to a fully-dressed Lipschitz and said, "You seemed to enjoy that."

"It's what it means to be alive," Lipschitz straightened his pale yellow necktie and gave her a peck on the lips.

"So, how do we get started? I wanna do this with you. Start a dungeon. I even looked online and I saw a place. It looks perfect. Let's take a look at it."

"Um. Okay. Yeah, let's do that," he responded.

"What about Chunxx?"

"She's been wanting to build her dream dungeon for years, but never had the cash, cause most of her money goes to her sick mother and to take care of her brain damaged kid. Let's include her. Why not? She knows the ropes, the clients, yeah. You got any extra cash?"

"Why don't we set up a meeting about that?" Georgia offered, "I may be able to make a significant contribution, assuming I could make money on my investment."

"Are you kidding? You could make a bundle. I'll write up a business plan, you can do the photography and be Chunxx's assistant. This has been my secret dream too, but don't tell my wife," he laughed.

"What about Harry?"

"Fuck Harry. What about him? He's a wimp and a loser."

"But he's still my boyfriend, and I think we both know that he knows about us."

"I'm your new boyfriend, Mistress Coco. You're my bitch and I'm yours. Get that through your pretty little head. You are gorgeous and talented. I appreciate and respect you, and he doesn't. You are done with this Harry asshole. Finished! Full stop! We are bullet proof! Do I have to punish you, sweet thing?"

"No, that's my game big boy, now bend over." She smacked him hard on the ass with her riding crop and laughed. "Now lick my shoes!"

Georgia relished this feeling of power, one she'd never known before, as he bent down, with alacrity, toward her shoes.

Chapter 23

Slender as a snake, like a slowly moving statue, unsmiling, unemotional, tight, smooth skin, a carefully manicured mons pubis, she gyrated ever so slowly, arms folded, then to the side, then hands clasped. She hoped someone was watching, maybe a neighbor, or the super or the exterminator or the bored day trader who looked up briefly from his computer and spied her across the airshaft. Georgia's curtains were wide open as she shared her nakedness with anyone who cared to look. Her camera snapped automatically, causing the strobe to flash every ten seconds.

The phone rang, a normal ring, not the electronic Mozart of Lipschitz's special ring. It was just Harry. She picked up the phone, saw it was him, and put it back down. She had no idea that he was downstairs, on the street, staring up at the apartment. He called three more times before she finally answered.

"Hey...it's me, I'm stranded down here on the street. Why didn't you pick up? never mind," Harry said "I saw the flashing strobe from the street." He wondered why she was ignoring him. "May I come up, mistress?" He inadvertently let the word slip.

Georgia briefly wondered why the fuck he called her *mistress*, then gave the doorman the okay to let him in. He knows, she thought, plus there was that little clue last night.

When Harry arrived at 34L, the door was already slightly open. She was naked, with her back to him. Always teasing, slightly bowlegged and scrawny, she bent over to turn off the strobe, exposing the pale rose of her anal sphincter and shaved labia. She languorously put on her flimsy, micro-mini, dark-blue kimono and intentionally left it open in the front. Her tough, artificial breasts bobbed slightly, preventing the robe from closing; her tight abdomen and a freshly shaven, barely bearded clam peered threateningly at Harry from beneath its closely cropped Hitler mustache of blonde pubic down.

"Have you been reading my emails!?" Georgia asked aggressively.

Harry entered the apartment, obediently removing his shoes. "No."

"How can you say that, you liar! You've been looking at them! Don't you fucking lie to me!" She spun around, lit a cigarette, and then took a swig from a half-filled tumbler of vodka. "Why did you whisper "Richard" into my ear last night?"

"I asked if you were *richer*," Harry lied, poorly.

"I'll ask you again: have you been reading my emails?"

"No!"

He knew he was busted. Actually, he wanted to be. Somehow, he thought that she would think he was quite clever, or a good criminal, or some kind of cool outlaw. Or maybe, if she knew she was in the company of a fellow liar, she would like him more than Richard Lipschitz, the social deviant she seemed to be in love with. You lie and so do I, he thought. We are perfect for each other. Can't you see? You don't need anyone else but me.

"Don't you stonewall me!" she said, angrily exhaling smoke into Harry's wide-eyed expression.

"Okay, yes. I know everything. I know his name, I know his wife's name, his dog's name, his kids' names. I know where he works, where he lives, his phone numbers, what his house looks like. Like God, I know everything."

Georgia turned away, toward the window, her flimsy kimono still wide open, as her neighbor the day trader got another eye full. Harry's eyes bugged and looked dangerous as she noticed that they pulled in every detail of her open kimono. She was furious now. She tossed the lit cigarette butt out the window, 34 floors above the sidewalk. "If you do anything to him, you will never see me, or hear from me, or find me again....*ever!* Fucking criminal! You are going to jail!" she wailed, growing more hysterical. "You are going now! I want you out! I can't stand you! You are FUCKED UP!"

"Fine, I'm leaving," Harry sputtered, losing his temper. "Fuck you back, bitch."

This hadn't gone quite as Harry had hoped. What *had* he hoped for? That she'd think he was cool, that he was clever to figure out what she'd been up to? Rueful, he realized he was hoping she'd think he was a genius for figuring it all out, and that she would fall in love with him.

He left, disappointed, hurt and angry—not because he'd been caught, but rather because he'd been misunderstood. And because he was now, possibly, really alone.

Georgia slammed the door behind him. She was furious, and the whole situation was Harry's fault. She was the victim here; she'd done nothing wrong. Plus, he could be a serious threat to Richard, now that he had gone to the trouble of a background check...

My sweet love...my sweet submissive mentor. Her empire of deception and protection had just crumbled before her eyes, now that Harry knew—and at least half the thrill was getting away with the deception. And most upsetting, she was losing control, her source of power. "FUCK!" She reached for her phone and got his voice mail. "Richard....we're busted. Harry knows everything." Shortly thereafter, with a ping, a new email arrived in Georgia's in-box.

From: Richard Lipschitz lipschitz@optonline.net
To: Georgia Pendleton g.nabokov@gmail.com
Subject: Harry

OK, so we are busted. You've been wanting to dump him anyway. Tell him you're gay, or at least that you're in no way, shape or form attracted to him. Here's a letter that I composed for you to send him.

Dear Harry,

Over the last ten years we have had good times and stressful times. Unfortunately the stressful times have caused me to write this letter. This letter is about me. My wants, needs and desires. Not about YOU.

I will be taking a break from you. For how long I do not know. I just cannot take it anymore. Our relationship is not what you want. I will not be changing my mind about getting back together as a couple. We will not be getting back together as a couple now, next month and next year or ever. That is the cold honest truth. I am done saying I am sorry. I am not. I need to move on with my life free from the stress you bring into my life. We both have done things we regret. That's all in the past. I have decided once and for all and will not be changing my mind about this. We will not be getting back together. You will have to find a way to deal with this decision. I need to move on with my life and cannot do so while maintaining any sort of relationship with you. Full stop. Now it's time for both of us to move on.

From: Georgia Pendleton g.nabokov@gmail.com
To: Richard Lipschitz lipschitz@optonline.net
Subject: Great letter

You are so funny... I'm gay and want to fuck women. Great letter BTW!!

Love, G

Chapter 24

Harry Waldheim's Journal

Problems occur when abused children grow up, or should I say reach a certain age, when they are expected to act as responsible adults. The tools and skills that they've acquired are extremely limited and function for only very specific circumstances, if at all. These poor creatures are, when left to their own devices, prone to self-destruction; and if two of them manage to develop a kind of bond or relationship, it is doomed from the outset to fail.

Chapter 25

Six-year-old, platinum haired, blue eyed Harry Waldheim; mostly ignored by the older boys, watched twelve-year-old Keith Cormia and his ten-year-old brother Michael lash a struggling, slimy, green, Leopard frog to an M-80 with a thin piece of copper wire. The firecracker was a half-inch in diameter and two inches long—a dense cardboard cylinder wrapped in brick red tissue, sealed at either end with a hard, wax-like substance. A stiff wick stuck straight up out of the middle of the cylinder. Harry knew the thing was more like a quarter stick of dynamite than a firecracker, and was really loud when it blew up. Keith, the older brother, grasped the frog and M-80 in one hand, then cleverly lit a match, using his other hand, by flicking his thumb and match head to the striker. He ignited the wick and hurled the struggling frog and quarter stick of dynamite high into the air.

Harry, eyes wide, thumbs in ears, witnessed the flash of white, a muffled blast and red flame. Dark gray smoke was all that remained of the frog, drifting in the breeze—that, and the unmistakable smell of gunpowder.

Harry stood near the entrance of 1011 Park Avenue. He held a newspaper and drank a hot cup of coffee, waiting. He suspected Richard

Lipschitz was either in there, on his way out, or on his way in from Connecticut to play hooky. He checked his cell phone out of habit, blending in with the other urban neurotics, alert and energized with the stress of getting to work and getting enough coffee to get through the morning. Aggressive yellow taxis dominated the streets. It was a cold, November morning—the chill echoed in the guarded movements of pedestrians exhaling puffs of steam. A cluster of pigeons flashed by overhead, and suddenly, there he was: Richard Lipschitz. He walked toward 1011 Park like Mister Cool himself. He strutted with grand arrogance. Delusional, he seemed to imagine himself king of the world. From a distance, one might assume he was an entitled, wealthy, financial sophisticate. From a distance, no one would notice that his camel-colored, wool trench coat was moth-eaten; his yellow tie, soiled; his dark, pinstripe suit unlaundered; and the heels of his scuffed, black, cordovan shoes were worn down at forty-five degree angles.

At a closer look, Richard Lipschitz might even have been mistaken for a penniless vagrant. Beyond his physical state, those dark, painfully sad eyes revealed an impoverished, neglected, abused and bullied child from Queens, whose only way of coping with his world was through a thick filter of denial, fantasy, delusion, and unbridled, insatiable greed.

Harry watched this sad fraud closing in on 1011 Park Avenue; his hatred dug its heels in deeper and deeper. "Lipschitz is a dead man," he growled, under his breath, and imagined closing in to intercept him as he neared the entrance to Georgia's building.

"Hey Dick....fucker," Harry imagined greeting Lipschitz from behind, putting his arm around his shoulder, hugging him tightly. Lipschitz squirms but can't escape without making a scene.

"Top of the morning to ya...fucker!" Harry kisses him on the cheek. "Do you know what sadism is?"

Lipschitz looks up, panicked.

"I do! I'm German!" Harry laughs, grabbing Lipschitz's head with both hands and kissing him quite hard on the lips. The kiss of death, Mafia style. Lipschitz squirms a bit more, but doesn't fight or try to defend himself. He truly is a pussy. Harry pulls back, slides his hands to the top of Lipschitz's head, and rips off his toupee, tossing it into the rush-hour traffic barreling down Park Ave. It flies away in ultra-slow motion, end over end, landing on the windshield of an oncoming taxi. The nonchalant driver flicks on the wipers, causing the toupee to fall off onto the street, where it is instantly run over by another taxi and sticks to the wheel for a few seconds until it flies off, landing in the center median on Park Ave, at the feet of a young boy. Eight-year-old Harry himself is waiting to cross with his mother, who is too preoccupied to notice as her son bends down to pick up this bit of fur, placing it on his head like a coonskin cap. As they cross the street, young Harry's mother looks down in horror and rips the new "hat" off her son's head, throwing it back out into the oncoming traffic, where it lands on another windshield...

Harry woke from his daydream just in time to observe Lipschitz enter Georgia's building with two large Starbuck's coffees. He greeted the doorman like an old friend and they exchanged guy hugs. Harry could faintly hear him ask about the wife and kid. He noted the doorman's smile as Lipschitz rushed through the lobby to the elevator.

Killing time, Harry sat at the counter at the diner across the street drinking a coffee and reading the Times. A copy of the Post lay just to his right.

The headline read, "Jealous Boyfriend Kills Ex-Girlfriend and Lover."

"Do you think that murder is ever justified?" Harry asked the total stranger sitting next to him. She was a middle-aged secretary, caffeinating for her eight hours of answering phones and serving the needs of her middle management boss, he assumed.

"Excuse me?" she gaped.

"This headline...do we really know what happened between these three victims? Maybe the lady and her new boyfriend were trying to drive the poor guy nuts. You know, gas light him, make him lose it, I mean."

"Well, rage..." she gathered her composure, attempting to finesse the potentially crazy person next to her.

Harry turned aggressively to her; she gets him, he thought. "Yeah, rage, animal survival, protecting the home. What about the military? Aren't they protecting the homeland? Isn't that the same...just on a macro level?"

"I don't want to get into this right now," she excused herself firmly and left in a hurry. Her retreat made him a bit calmer, but he turned his manic attention to the waitress and asked, "Have you ever been in love?"

"I'm not sure," she responded. She'd seen far worse nutcases.

Another woman sitting next to Harry moved away, avoiding eye contact, but Harry was oblivious to the actions of those around him.

Harry entered the building about a half hour after Lipschitz. He and the doorman nodded to one another, distantly. He passed through the dark wood paneled lobby, reminiscent of a thrift shop version of a WASPy old men's club: strange pieces of 60's modern couches, chairs and tables juxtaposed at odd angles, a large brass urn with an arrangement of artificial flowers. A group of blue-haired old ladies chatted, in Yiddish, in front of a menorah and some ancient Christmas ornaments that "decorated" the fake fireplace and mantle. The guy at the front desk, skin white as a florescent light bulb, glanced up for a split second and then continued reading his New York Post, holding up the headline: Jealous Boyfriend Kills Ex-Girlfriend and Lover.

Harry rode up to the 34th floor next to some stinky, fat guy. They exchanged uncomfortable smiles as Harry exited. As he walked down the hallway toward 34L, taking her key out of his pocket, he heard their muffled voices on the other side of the door and paused to listen.

"You gotta get him where it counts...in the pocket book, or send him to jail. Look...you can report him to the IRS or the FBI or the CIA...whatever.

"Good idea." Harry heard her barely audible agreement through the closed door.

He put the key in the lock, mumbling aloud, under his breath. "Hmmm. Here we go...entering Fucking-him Palace. Here's Johnny..."

Harry blasted the door open. Georgia and Lipschitz, curled up on the couch, looked up, startled. Harry was more than a little pleased with himself to see that Lipschitz seemed genuinely afraid for his pathetic, pig life. Without removing his shoes (a very strict rule in Georgia's household) Harry marched across the room toward the two lovebirds. Georgia jumped up and, with greater force than one could imagine a petite woman capable of, she shoved Harry back, stopping his forward movement. He stumbled a bit, and ended up slamming down in a nearby chair-

-where Lipschitz's laptop computer happened to be. The loud crack, as the screen shattered, added to the tension.

"Harry! What the fuck are you doing?" she screamed.

"I guess I should be going now," Lipschitz suggested in the pretend voice of a frightened child.

"No, I really think you should stay," countered Harry.

"Listen, I don't have any money. I'm broke," responded Lipschitz, actually opening his tattered wallet to show that it contained no cash.

"Money? What are you talking about?" asked Harry.

Harry stood facing the two in silence. He wondered why the hell Lipschitz would bring up money. Did this idiot think he was trying to extort money for his silence? That he was going to let him off that easily?

"You are the epitome of everything that's wrong with this world. Do you need to own everything you see? Can't get enough. You're a human cash register, you fat, doughnut-eating, slime-sucking swine. You disgust me!" Harry vented as he confronted his arch enemy. He felt the words flow out of his mouth like fists—one to the solar-plexis, a right upper-cut, then a left cross to the liver. He scored a knock-down in their first meeting in the ring.

Lipschitz silently nodded, realizing that he probably wouldn't be killed, at least not right away. He declared, with side-stepping arrogance, "People have affairs all the time. It's no big deal."

"You vile scum. Easy for you to say. At least you have a fat, loyal wife and three children who love you unconditionally. You'll get up and leave here and go back to a loving home. I will, thanks to you, have nothing but a broken life and a future of solitude." Truly feeling sorry for himself, he looked away. I guess this is really the end of Georgia and me, Harry thought.

"Don't bring my family into this," Lipschitz said, standing up to defend his family with self-righteous indignation.

"Never mind that. Get off your high horse, family man. Go back to the burbs, back to number 1 Gorge and Gulch Lane, or wherever the fuck you live, and climb back on that ride mower, fat man!"

Lipschitz wondered how Harry knew about his fat wife and three kids. And his address—or some facsimile of his address. This guy really was dangerous. He took a deep breath and pondered his only exit.

Harry watched Lipschitz's eyes travel to the front door, where his shoes were obediently lined up in the foyer. Harry spun around, reached over, grabbed one of the shoes, and—in one fluid, unhinged motion—flipped it out the window of 34L He imagined it falling in ultra, slow motion as it arced out and down, end over end.

Georgia and Lipschitz ran to the window and looked out to see the shoe slam to the street below, just in front of a moving taxi. They gaped as it was immediately run over and then bounced under another vehicle—and another, and another, until it reached the other side of Park Avenue and came to rest in the gutter. They watched, blinking, as a homeless woman, pushing a grocery cart, piled with cans, bent over, picked up the shoe, tossed it into her cart, and moved on.

What the fuck, mouthed Georgia? Harry could see her internal struggle, fighting back feelings of both anger and amusement.

Harry was still ragingly mad, but he had to laugh at the irony of his toupee fantasy and the actual shoe on the street taking part in rush hour traffic reality. Soon, he was cackling like a psychopath at what he'd just done, at the line he'd crossed.

"What the fuck?" shouted Lipschitz. "Well, I can see that I'm just a pawn here, and I'm leaving now. I hope I never see either of you two again. Ever." He got up, obviously afraid, yet feigning indignation, straightened his yellow necktie, slipped on his one remaining shoe, put on his moth-eaten camel coat, picked up his broken laptop, and limped out the door. Harry noticed a large hole in the heel of Lipschitz's sock as the door slowly closed. After a minute of silent rage, Georgia growled, "Leave. Now! What the fuck, Harry?! Get out! I need some time and space to think!"

"You sound like a broken record, needing to be alone. Needing time and space. You're never alone."
"Fuck you," Harry.

Chapter 26

As the Metro North train pulled out of Grand Central Station, Richard Lipschitz breathed a sigh of relief. Settling into his seat, eyes closed, he reflected on the events of the past hour. Yes, he thought, he was always the victim—his favorite position, one he coveted. His current position was much like being bound, ball-gagged, wrapped in Saran, mummified, hoisted upside down, spat on, whipped, and hosed. A broad smile crept over his spray-tanned head and it bobbed as the train rose from underground caverns, into daylight above ground. In a world of his own, he was oblivious to the thinly packed train as it pulled north to the first stop: Harlem, 125th Street. He gazed out the window at the passing scenery: train tracks, graffiti, trash, beer bottles, plastic scraps, old tires, a dead pickup truck, a cluster of hobos living under a bridge, ragged blue tarps piled over sticks and plywood shards. He pulled out his small flask and swigged, the alcohol warming as it entered his blood stream. The fun was just beginning, he mused, head nodding with the rhythmic movement of the train. His phone blared the cheesy Mozart's concerto in C# major.

"Where are you? You okay? I'm really sorry about Harry and his bull-shit...he's out of control... I can handle him, but I think we should do this together."

Dick rambled into his Blackberry, staring blankly out the window as the scenery whizzed by in a blur. "Yeah, I know, he's potentially very dangerous to me. I have a few acquaintances who would be more than happy to make his life miserable. You have to tell me what his weaknesses are and where he's most vulnerable. How can we cause him to go broke and crazy at the same time. Undermine his investments, steal his clients if he has any, discredit him among his friends and network, get him evicted from his rent-stabilized loft."

Lipschitz was on a manic high from all the conflict as he continued his dive into problem solving mode, not letting Georgia get a word in.

"I'm beginning to love this. Let's destroy this asshole before he destroys us! Lead him on. Make him think you care about him, you know, then dump him, and then lead him on again. He's obsessed with you. Tease his cock, then walk away. I'll figure out what we can do to him legally for hacking into our emails and I'll do a complete background check. Does he have a criminal record, or own any guns? I'm loving this and loving you even more now. Let's talk at our usual 9:30 tonight. I'll be walking the dog, rain or shine." He clicked off the Blackberry, shoving it in his inside pocket, then looked down at his feet in the new jogging sneakers.

"Throwing my shoe out the window, he chuckled to himself, "that's a first."

Lipschitz took another swig from his flask, his eyes at two-o-clock. She was in her late twenties, entering the train at Pelham. He was on her like a birddog, making mental notes. Five feet six inches barefoot, but five-nine in those black leather over-the-knee stilettos. Very refined, he noticed, with La Perla fishnets beneath her leather micro-mini. Maybe she was a stripper or possibly a high end sex worker. She definitely worked out, with that firm, slim ass. He appreciated the ironic mock, mod, wide belt over her dark brown leather Westcott. A little too obvious, maybe, with that thin, leather choker against her pale porcelain neck, punked-out Pepé Le Pew hair, and those French tip manicured fingernails. "All the better to bugger me with, my dear," he said, sotto voce. Convinced that she was a player in the lifestyle, just like him, his cock began to swell. He undressed her mentally—slowly—one button, one zipper, one lace at a time.

"Tickets please." The buff, young conductor snapped him out of his fantasy. Lipschitz looked up, digging into his back pocket, and pulled out his beat up wallet. A new fantasy gathered as his eyes slowly moved up the crease of the charcoal grey uniform next to him. He imagined muscular, shaved quadriceps then pausing, ever so skillfully and briefly—possibly uncircumcised, his fantasy continued, with a six-pack, of course. Handing the conductor his commuter card, he thought to himself: James Dean, Marlin Brando and Brad Pitt. Now there's a face that could only be improved with my cock in its mouth.

Chapter 27

For most of their adult lives, both Harry and Georgia had been spo-
radically under the watchful eyes of all manner of psychiatrists, psy-
chologists, psycho-pharmacologists, couples counselors, gurus,
faith healers and spirit guides. They knew they were almost always in
need of some type of advice and counsel and quite often sought it out.
But, in addition, they both chose to self-medicate. Georgia's drug of
choice was alcohol and Harry's Ambien. Just a little something to stop
the madness, Harry told himself.

On her last visit to see Violet, her new therapist, Georgia talked a lot
about her current threesome—being careful, of course, not to mention
the kinkier aspects of her relationship with Richard. Violet suggested
couple's counseling, since Georgia and Harry had been together for such
a long time. Georgia decided to act on this advice of her most recent
therapist. The suggestion was: End this in a civilized manner, you may
even find that you still have things in common and actually still love and
respect each other. Georgia figured there was nothing to lose.

It was a cold January evening when Georgia and Harry arrived at the
unlit entrance of Doctor Gladstone's office, all the way west on 104th
Street and Riverside Drive. They climbed the stairs and, not finding a
buzzer, knocked loudly on the outside door. After a minute, or so, they
heard a commotion inside that sounded like furniture being rearranged.
Ten seconds later, an extremely large, dark haired, middle aged, bearded

man poked his head out and welcomed them inside. He explained that the door they had been knocking on hadn't locked in years, thus the piles of furniture in front of it. Doctor Gladstone gestured for them to sit, pointing first to an old aluminum beach chair for Harry and then to the "comfortable" chair for Georgia, which seemed to have been dragged in off the street and only had a few remnants of upholstery clinging to its decrepit frame. Doctor Gladstone sat in the only piece left, a relatively intact Barcalounger.

Dr. Gladstone's *office* could not possibly have had more stuff inside it: three television sets were stacked in front of one another. (One had to assume the one in front was the current working model.) Harry made a conservative estimate that there were 5,000 VHS tapes piled on top of one another, at least 3,000 books and possibly 10,000 magazines, all without the benefit of a single shelf to hold them. The remainder of the studio apartment brimmed with clothing and furniture and endless black plastic garbage bags bulging with who knew what, to such an extent that Harry had to literally walk sideways to move in any limited direction. The apartment was the very definition of a hoarder's paradise.

Harry surreptitiously depressed the record button on his hidden MP3 recorder, a new tool in his spying arsenal. Moments later, they were midway through the doctor's intake questions.

"Propranolol, clonazepam, Lexapro, Ambien," stated Harry.

"I take that too," nodded Georgia, as she considered bolting for the exit, only remaining out of duty to her real motive: obeying her dear submissive, Richard. *Lead him on and make him think you still want to be together, then pull away. Do this until he goes nuts.*

"I just need a very general idea of what you're taking. Is there anything else? Have either of you ever been in therapy before, extensively or otherwise?

"Yes," confirms Georgia. Violet referred us to you.

Harry said, "Yes, my most recent therapist, Annie Liebling, has suggested that I return as soon as possible considering current events."

"Of course. Okay, let's get down to why you are here. Georgia?"

"Okay... A little over a month ago, well we'd been having some ups and downs. And, I can only speak for myself, but I've been unhappy, and have not had enough... I'm not having much fun," she began. "We don't live together. I felt unacknowledged and was having a hard time communicating. I wasn't being listened to. He doesn't listen."

"So you felt that you were expressing what you wanted to say, but it wasn't getting across."

"Yeah, yeah...uhh. Oh, it's not that there weren't a lot of positive feelings between us, but there was a real problem with communication. Maybe I should have tried harder to work things out with Harry, but Richard just fell into my life. And I, ummmm, so...a month and a half ago, I started seeing this other guy."

"For the first time?"

"Yes. And Harry found out about it, and I—which was horrible—and I—I realized that I had to make a change in my relationship—with Harry."

"How did Harry find out?"

Harry refrained from interrupting and merely shook his head while he seethed in self-pity and anger.

"I think Harry suspected that I was seeing somebody else. I went to a football game with this other guy and Harry didn't believe my story, because I lied about why I was going and with whom. Harry called my friend Becky—that's who I said I was going with—and found out that I lied. And then he sort of broke into my emails." Georgia paused and glanced over at Harry who had the slightest smile on his face. It was actually a little creepy, but when she looked again, his face was back to its blank, listening mode. "And he found out about my relationship with this other guy. But I was having real communication problems with Harry. See? He just doesn't listen."

Dr. Gladstone focused on Georgia, and cleaned his glasses. "One big problem with many couples is called mind reading. That's where we assume we know what the other person is thinking. And then we react to something that doesn't even exist, or react inappropriately to something that perhaps wasn't an issue at all. It's clear that this is happening here."

"I don't think that either of us communicates very well," she responded.

"Well, let me ask you this. You've been having an affair, and maybe this is still going on. What is it that you want to accomplish here? Do you want to end the relationship? Do you want to find a way to close it? What is it that you want to accomplish here?"

Georgia found Dr. Gladstone tedious and imposing. Her only defense was to drift off and think happy, pleasant, soothing thoughts. These questions were much too direct for Georgia and she descended into the safety of a daydream.

She and Lipschitz are lying on her couch. She is on top, naked. He is wearing only a woman's blouse and his hands are bound with red climbing rope.

"Don't worry my little Gomez, you're safe with me. I won't let Harry harm you. We'll destroy him together."

Snapping out of it after a moment, she finally responded. "Well I have to say that I'm not really sure what I want. I can't really think clearly. I don't even know how I'm feeling. I need time and space. I'm having trouble, you know, loving myself. I have no business in a relationship anyway," squirmed Georgia.

"Well, that's problematic, because you're not ready to be in a relationship, but you've been in one for..." He looked at Harry for confirmation.

"Nine years," said Harry.

"Nine years. And now you are having an affair," stated Gladstone, getting right down to business.

Finally, Harry spoke up. "If I could just say one thing. Dr. Gladstone turned toward Georgia and she nodded. "This was not just an average affair. This was the beginning of a relationship, and not just an average vanilla relationship. This was a sadomasochistic, bondage and discipline sort of relationship. And it wasn't like they had a couple of one-night stands. They went on trips together. They have been making plans... It is beyond my comprehension that my best friend would do this to me."

"If I might," Gladstone interrupted. "When something like this happens, it comes as a shock to the person who was betrayed. Often that person will ask, *What did I do? How could this be?* The conscious mind asks those questions, because our unconscious mind drives us to think that we don't understand what we're really doing. Georgia, you were saying that you had all these frustrations building up, and yet you feel that you might have tried even harder, rather than having an affair. Tried harder at what? What was going on with you?"

Floundering, and looking desperate, Georgia lied, "Yes, the affair was turning into a relationship, but it wasn't based on BDSM or SM or whatever you want to call it."

Georgia drifted back to her daydream.

Lipschitz is wearing his blond wig, adult diapers, nipple clamps and nothing else. He is in Georgia's living room, dancing clumsily to a Casio version of Elton John's "I'm Still Standing." Georgia coaches him like an aerobics instructor: lift those legs higher, flex those arms, work those abs. Now side...and side...and back...and back. Georgia cracks a bull whip. She is wearing fringed leather chaps open in back and front, cowboy boots, elbow-high leather gloves, a black leather cop's hat, and nothing else.

She smiled at the thought.

Harry looked at her and wondered what was going on.

His gaze snapped her back to the therapy session, but her brain was slow to come to the task at hand, "That was just not really part of our relationship. I never had an affair or a relationship that took place in a dungeon..."

"Um-hmmm...okay," mused Gladstone. He was getting the picture that there would be plenty to unfold in this couple's many layers and in Georgia's probably borderline personality.

Frustrated, Harry looked directly at Georgia, and asked "Do you think you've done anything wrong?"

"I don't know," she mumbled, avoiding any eye contact.

"My question really is *do you know right from wrong?*" drilled Harry, hoping to gain the sympathy of Doctor Gladstone.

"No, I'm a psychopath. Hee, hee—I'm a psychopathic killer. Hah," giggled Georgia, resorting to sarcasm.

"This is a serious question," stated Gladstone.

Harry couldn't take it anymore. A flood of self-righteous anger overtook him.

"I looked you in the eye. I gave you every opportunity to tell me and confess to me and to talk to me about this. You looked me in the eye countless times and said *no.*" Harry glanced at Gladstone, whose eyes were closed while he shook his head slightly from side to side. He took that as a vote of confidence, whether it was meant that way, or not, and continued. "You said, 'I'm not doing anything. There's nobody else.' And then, when you found out that I knew, the first thing you said to me was, 'If you do anything to him, you will never see me, or speak to me, or hear from me again....ever!'"

Harry stared at Georgia, watching her fall farther and farther away from him. His sorrow was deeper than his anger. His breathing became slow and erratic. "You protected him then, and you're protecting him now, in this room," he went on. "All of your vagueness, indecision, and feigned agony are all about creating a subterfuge in order to rebuild your fetishistic empire of lies and deception. When I walked in on you two in that room, I walked toward you. The first thing you did was to charge toward me and push me away. You shoved me in the chest with all your might. You were protecting the man you love, and you and Lipschitz are out to intentionally annihilate me. So, I'm asking you again, do you know right from wrong?"

"Noooooo!!!!!!" she screamed. Not just a scream—a sound blasted from this petite, slender woman almost beyond the threshold of human hearing and understanding. It rose from her lungs, diaphragm, and solar plexus, but also from parts ancient, forgotten, and unknown—from the depths of her cranium and soul. It was eardrum-collapsing. Harry and Gladstone looked at each other, wide-eyed and a little afraid.

Harry silently implored Gladstone with a glance that said *Now do you understand what and who I am dealing with?*

Gladstone answered in silence, with a nod, *I get it, pal.* Then he said out loud, "I think it's time we end this session and schedule something for next week."

Georgia agreed to return.

Why would she agree to continue therapy? wondered Harry. *I guess she wants to continue this torture..?*

Chapter 28

Harry Waldheim's Journal

The tension of a triangle creates a structure, feeding and dependent on the adjacent parts to be complete. There is no love here; no kindness, no sympathy, no empathy. Instead, a selfish and insatiable need to be satisfied and to maintain the illusion of having power and control....to what end? For what reason? This is a senseless, meaningless slaughter; a brilliant display of the lowest levels of human interaction. Three players, three legs of a triangle, wallowing in slime, gouging and scratching, face biting, castrating, ass fucking, cock sucking, disemboweling and decapitating.

Chapter 29

Back in the middle nineties, when Sarah and Richard Lipschitz had been married only a few years, they bought Number One Knoll n' Gorge Drive with money that Sarah had inherited from her grandmother. They paid cash, got a good deal, and saw their equity skyrocket. Sixteen years later, every house but theirs had been torn down and replaced. The three bedroom split-level appeared tiny and lost in a ghetto of giant, supersized, overstuffed, garish McMansions.

When they first bought the house, the happy couple, very much do-it-yourselfers, became obsessed with painting and decorating in spite of their tight budget. Pier One and Ikea became major elements of the décor, with an occasional splurge on Ethan Allen. Beiges and browns, with a splash here and there of colored silk flowers, completed their interpretation of good taste and opulence. In those days, a younger and leaner Richard, actually had a regular job as a financial planner at the local Bucksport Trust Company. He would come home from work and dive into one of his many home repair projects. No job too small, he used to joke, as he changed light bulbs, filled, spackled and painted walls and trim, lubricated drawer slides, door hinges and aluminum storms and screens. "Chores-chores-chores," he happily chirped. He built a basement workshop, complete with a workbench and pegboard to organize his small assortment of hand tools. He got into woodworking. Sarah bought him a subscription to *Popular Woodworking*, which featured a monthly assortment of simple projects for the handy man: a wooden toothbrush holder, a toolbox, a shoeshine kit, a decorative novelty mailbox.

"Turn your common everyday mailbox into a real conversation piece: a golden retriever," he read. This was the project for him, and with the encouragement of his loving wife, thus began the mailbox project. With his new Black and Decker saber saw he cut out the four legs, then the head and tail, following the simple instructions and patterns. He carefully sanded the edges of the three-quarter inch white pine perfectly smooth, then applied one coat of primer and two coats of tan exterior latex paint. Finally he fastened all the wooden parts to a brand new steel United States postal regulation mailbox, before mounting it on the post at the end of the driveway. He proudly glued on the plastic number 1, then "Knoll n' Gorge Lane," then "The Lipschitz Residence" and then stood back. So proud of himself, he beamed and pondered the approval and amazement of his neighbors.

Fifteen years later, those neighbors were long gone, bought out by commodities traders, derivatives sharks, quants, CEOs and hedge fund managers. The Lipschitz family was the only one in the neighborhood without a fully-staffed grounds keeping crew.

Now, the golden retriever mailbox is missing a leg and a few letters in the name and address, and is in bad need of a paint job. Dick and Sarah have three children, Dick is bald, and he and his wife have not had sex with each other since before their youngest child was born. Dick is now an unemployable, drunken, cheating loser, too broke to leave his wife and delusional about his role as a family man. He still considers himself the lord of the manor, in spite of his wife making ends meet with stipends from a modest inheritance and a few private accounting clients.

Saturday morning, the day after his encounter with Harry at Georgia's apartment, found Dick already drunk and mowing the lawn. It was a cold winter day, although there had been no snow yet. Obviously, there wasn't much of a lawn to cut, but out of habit, and lack of imagination, the lord of the manor straddled his decrepit mower, which was on its last legs and spewing dark grey smoke. A can of beer in one hand and an unlit, chewed up soggy cigar in the other, Dick steered mostly with his knees, mowing erratically, back and forth, circling a neglected shrub, barely missing the ice encrusted birdbath, leaving patches of uncut lawn, like a bad haircut. Chopped up bits of paper, tennis balls and eviscerated plastic toys were strewn in his wake. He sang some Country/Western song off key, at the top of his voice.

"*And I drive ..drive, drive, drive...*

Trying to get back home...

Just a cowboy driving all alone..."

It was a cold, sunny, beautiful fall day, and the three Lipschitz siblings—Bruce, 16, Rachael, 14 and Jessica, 12, were hermetically sealed in the darkened living room with the dust encrusted brown drapes pulled shut. They were lost to the world of video games, absorbed completely. Invisible to them were the threadbare, overstuffed, brown and beige upholstered chairs and sofa, stuffing spewing from cuts and gashes suffered from years of the children's battles, food fights, projectile snot and vomit. On the walls, where once carefully framed and placed family portraits proudly hung, only a few remained, cracked and forlorn. For years the living room suffered the impact of all manner of wooden blocks, plastic fire trucks, Barbie dolls, and projectiles, both soft and hard, thrown in battle. Its contents barely survived the three children, now in their teens, who sat in virtual darkness, illuminated only by the moving images on the flat screen. A subwoofer tossed deep sounds of artillery canons around with more realism than actual combat. The children concentrated as though their lives depended on it.

In the kitchen, a million miles away from the battlefield in the once painstakingly decorated living room, Sarah Lipschitz and her parents were preparing lunch.

"Where did you say you were going on vacation dear?" Sarah's mom screamed, having to compete with the nasal drone of The Ellen Show blaring from a television balanced on top of the recipe-decoupaged refrigerator, the sounds of the kids fighting world war three in the living room, and the roaring lawn mower strafing the side of the house, inebriated Dick Lipschitz at the helm.

"Mom, I think I told you, Dick and the kids and I are going to Myrtle Beach later this spring. Should be fun. He needs a break. He works so hard. I don't know what he does all day, I almost never see him, but when I do he's always exhausted." Sarah opened the refrigerator. It was crammed to capacity with snacks, half-gallon jugs of soda, beer and leftovers. She pulled out a dozen eggs packed in Styrofoam, closing the door with her corpulent hind quarters, then shoved the debris of pots, pans and junk food aside, carving out a small island of counter top. From this tiny niche, she proceeded to crack a dozen eggs to make a cheese omelet for the family's lunch.

The sound of the mower echoed as Lipschitz swerved sharply into the garage which was cluttered with bikes, kayaks, skis, overflowing garbage cans and the results of too many drunken trips to Wal-Mart. *Can't find the rake? We'll just buy another one.* Scraps of leaves and twigs blew over the cement floor as he killed the engine, still clasping the soaked stogie in his hand. He pounded the remaining half can of beer in his other hand with one swift chug and threw the empty toward the "recycling area." He missed, but what the fuck? He was the lord of his manor. He covered the monthly nut, at least in his imagination. "Let someone else clean up this mess," he drunkenly mused aloud.

Lippy built his basement sanctum sanctorum after his second daughter was born, twelve years ago. He designed and built the room himself, and was still quite proud of his accomplishment. Most importantly, he put in a strong metal door with a sturdy lock, to which he possessed the only key. Without exception, he was the only human allowed in. Jack, the family's labradoodle, however, was always allowed, but he could only be lured in with food, and couldn't wait to leave as soon as he was finished scarfing down whatever leftover pizza or submarine sandwich was offered. The door's inside was covered in scratch marks and paw prints made by a desperate Jack attempting to escape the cigar fumes and dense mold spore contamination of the sacred man cave.

"C'mon buddy...have a treat," Lipschitz coaxed, bending over with a scrap of pizza crust as a lure.

"C'mon...that's it." The lure always seems to work on the sweet, unsuspecting pooch, as Jack reluctantly entered and Lipschitz slammed the door shut. He fell onto the couch, TV remote in hand, and surfed the channels on the old, oversized set, rescued from the living room. The lights were low and the room was mostly illuminated by the glow of the television screen and Jack was already scratching to get out.

Paneling the walls over the cement block foundation had been the least expensive way to transform a basement into a "finished" room. The only tiny window, which let very little natural light into the space, hadn't been cleaned, perhaps, ever. The drop ceiling, that Lipschitz painstakingly installed several years ago, housed four fluorescent light fixtures, quite bright when they all worked, but now several of the bulbs were dying and tended to flicker at random intervals. The room was strewn with papers—mostly neglected, unfinished work and dog-eared sports magazines. An old, used laptop sat, encrusted with grime, on a desk made from an old door and two sawhorses. The bookshelves, made of unfinished yellow pine boards, were mostly empty and warped. A couple of high school wrestling trophies, a photograph from twelfth grade, when he still had a full head of real mod hair, and a mostly empty bottle of Jack Daniels completed the decor, along with a couch, beaten up beyond repair and a threadbare shag rug, a remnant from the master bedroom, completed the decor.

A cheap handheld memo audio recorder sat on the couch next to a spiral notebook. Lippy picked up the recorder, clicked record, and spoke in a controlled drunken cadence. "Hi, it's me again, and what a week we've had on Wall Street. In spite of the volatility we're seeing in the market these days, I'm convinced that we will come out ahead of the game. But in this game we need a plan and a strategy so that we can move the needle and continue to grow as a team, and as a group of relationship teams. Let's expand our horizons and understand what the firm has to offer outside of your specific area, because that's what our clients expect. What can you bring to the table that will help solve their issues?" He paused, then flashed his giant capped teeth. "Until next time...."

Satisfied that his pearls of wisdom had been recorded for the archive, he passed out in an inebriated heap on the sad remains of the sofa, TV blaring, Jack scratching and whimpering. He was out cold until dinnertime.

From: Richard Lipschitz lipschitz@optonline.net
To: Georgia Pendleton gnabokov@gmail.com
Subject: Conference Opportunity

Friday May 5th in Stanford at the Westin Hotel there is a celebrity conference starring Donald Trump. The topics are real estate, how to cut capital gains, protecting your assets from lawsuits and divorce. I have two tickets and you can get Trump's book for free.

Master Gomez

From: Georgia Pendleton gnabokov@gmail.com
To: Richard Lipschitz lipschitz@optonline.net
Subject: Conference Opportunity

Cool....I would love to go!!
    Xxxxxxxxxxx

Chapter 30

The aphrodisiac of secrecy—of pulling the wool over some unsuspecting lover's eyes, getting away with lies, fucking in public—these petty crimes and cheap thrills gave profound meaning to the lives of Richard and Georgia. But they enriched the life of Harry, as well. They continued living on the edge, hiding behind the curtains, away from Lipschitz's wife and children and Georgia's boyfriend, or so they thought. They imagined they were undetected, free from unpleasant consequences even as, invisibly, Harry watched their every move, having hacked into their new, recently altered, internet identities.

Without missing a beat, he continued to surreptitiously observe many a secret rendezvous at fancy restaurants, motels, beds and breakfasts, on trains, and on and on. Once, in his favorite Rasta disguise, he watched them fuck at a movie theater. They sat in the last row in some multiplex on 42nd Street, she on his lap, facing forward, he holding the popcorn, pretending to nibble. Harry sat way off to one side, back to the wall, and watched the two copulate in public. It took every bit of self-control he could muster to keep from smashing them both. They thought they were getting away with something, the fools. On several occasions he observed them taking flip cam videos of themselves in flagrante delicto; making great art, or so they thought, he imagined. He was amazed at the extent to which they were self-deceiving masters of their assumed-to-be-private universe. And all the while, Harry looked on.

Over the course of many months of clandestine operations, the demise of Richard Lipschitz was always on his mind. A quiet spike to the kidney in some dark alley; a wire noose from behind, wrapped tightly around the neck; Harry waiting patiently in the dark, back seat of the leased Lexus SUV, leaving his inebriated victim surprised and gasping for his last bits of air; and of course, the Taser option, with its allure of slow torture. He'd thought of countless endings for his rival.

Often, following them wasn't even necessary as Harry, through the course of his obsessive research, came across the ever changing and brutal website of Mistress Chunxx. It was as though they really wanted the world to understand, and maybe even embrace, what they were doing. *At least accept us as the artists we really are*, they seemed to beckon through their many posts on the Chunxx website. There were numerous videos of the five foot one inch tall chubby mistress, looking much like a pink beach ball stuffed into (and overflowing out of) a black leather corset, her stubby, fat legs barely able to walk in thigh-high, black, vinyl stilettos, always with the ubiquitous black leather, Marlon Brando, biker cap teetering on the back of her blond, nylon coiffure. Collagen inflated, puffed, bright red lips and giant, circular, dark plastic sun goggles completed her look. All-in-all, she was a fairly good imitation of an obese, inflatable, sex doll.

One such video took place in Atlantic City as they geared up for Chunxx's self-published, co-authored (i.e. ghostwritten) book launch. This video also found her introducing none other than Georgia as her assistant, referring to her as "my little Dior." Georgia obediently fumbled an awkward, "Hi, I'm Dior." after being coached to, "introduce yourself, Dear."

Lipschitz was along for the ride as well this time, as the videographer. His muffled voice could be heard coaxing and directing Georgia to look sexy, do a twirl, and blow a kiss. She wore the same black vinyl boots as Chunxx, but instead of a corset she was dressed in a threadbare black slip. She must have pulled that out of her mother's closet or some thrift shop at the last minute, Harry thought. As she spun for the camera, looking like some crazed granny, one of her breasts popped out, the thin strap falling off her shoulder. Too drunk to notice, she continued her performance as Mistress Chunxx droned on.

"Hi, we're here in beautiful downtown Atlantic City." (They could be in any Ramada Inn luggage holding area anywhere in the world, Harry thought.) "Getting ready for the first signing of my new book, *The Manual of Domestic Domination,* here at Club Kink. We're very much looking forward to this, and it could not have happened without the help of my fabulous manager, Dior, and I want everyone to meet her."

Lipschitz panned right to a medium shot of Georgia. Harry squinted at the screen, taking in her fuzzy, bleached blond, Phyllis Diller hair and more mascara than Harry had ever seen on her. Her face, recently tightened, gave her an unwrinkled and numb, unmoving upper lip. Same went for her forehead. She smiled a vast, forced smile for the camera, revealing newly capped and polished front teeth. She pulled her thin shoulder strap back in place, covering her exposed boob.

"Hi-eee," she grinned, suppressing obvious fear of being interviewed on camera. "I'm Dior...." She looked directly into the lens, dark eyes wide, attempting a sexy expression. "I manage the fabulous Mistress Chunxx." The camera pulled back to show Georgia's hands on her hips in a fashion model pose as she swiveled around in her ratty slip, mugging for the camera. In the background, Harry noted beige walls, fake marble, and a couple of tired luggage carts—grim reminders of the back door of the afore mentioned Ramada Inn service exit.

Dior stumbled through her lines. "Club Kink has graciously invited us to do a book signing with their Saturday night opening, and there'll be crowds and crowds, so please come." She looked like a tongue tied deer, frozen in headlights but Chunxx saved the day by chiming in, "And doesn't Dior look hot?" which prompted Georgia to do a few more twirls, as her normal frown began to seep through the fake smile.

"Who could possibly have a hotterr managerrr," Chunxx gushed, trying to pump up the mood. "If she doesn't open doors for me, who else can?" Chunxx grabbed Georgia, giving her a giant fat lady kiss on the cheek. "I love my Dioorr!"

There were many more videos on the Chunxx website, and Harry was headed right down the rabbit hole: Lipschitz, wearing a hood, getting paddled onstage at some anonymous club, Chunxx strapped and stuffed into an extra-large corset, by Georgia as she struggled with the laces, cigarette dangling from her lower lip (she was wearing the same shabby black slip), Chunxx facing some middle-aged fat guy, arms tied behind his back.

She smoked a cigarette and spit on his face and in his mouth, then ordered him to expose his tongue so she could perform her signature move, twisting the cigarette out on it as the sad gimp quivered in agony and ecstasy. In another, Chunxx sat on a couch wearing a bright blue strap-on dildo. Lipschitz, wearing a pink miniskirt and blond wig, drunkenly crawled on all fours toward her and began going down on the dildo, groaning loudly. (Evidently, Georgia directed and shot this one, as her voice could be heard crooning from behind the camera, "Take it all, big boy. That's it Gomez, worship that cock.")

In a final shot, Chunxx lay comfortably on her back, in her darkened boudoir, seductively facing the camera and blew cigarette smoke toward the lens. She looked like a bloated Nancy Sinatra, brittle blond hair, raccoon mask of eye makeup, and sex doll collagen filled lips.

"Enough for today," Harry sighed, and shut down his computer.

He used a simple hack on her cell phone that allowed him to pinpoint her exact longitude and latitude. This made it easy for him to arrive at the scene, often before even Georgia and Richard. He'd usually go incognito—sometimes just a hoodie pulled over his face, other times fake beards and hippie hair, and sometimes he'd even darken his skin with makeup. Sunglasses were de rigueur. He never got caught, being ever so patient as he followed them to their secret meetings in fancy restaurants, bars, business events. He even trailed them to a Bernie Madoff cocktail party once, where Lipschitz worked the room, trolling for any kind of business connection possible, while Georgia pretended to be socially at ease and proceeded to get very drunk.

Eventually they'd glance up at each other, give the nod, and meet in the men's room, a closet, or some empty bedroom and lock the door. Harry could just imagine Dick lifting up his shirt and lowering his pants to the floor as Georgia instructed. In his mind's eye, he could see the clothes pins covering Lipshitz's chest, penis and testicles. She'd yank and twist them and force him to sit in the urinal as she spat in his mouth and force fed him her cigarette butt.

Once, in yet another movie theater, Harry was able to sit invisibly behind them and watch as Lipschitz placed a container of popcorn on his lap, poking his dick up through a hole in the bottom so that it was surrounded by popcorn. Georgia dug into the container while keeping her eyes on the screen. He saw her hand moving up and down in the container but she never seemed to bring any popcorn up to her mouth. Finally, he saw her reach into her handbag, with her free hand, and pull out a large clothespin. With his earphones in and a directional mic hidden in a rolled up newspaper, he could hear her as she clamped it on his erection and instructed him to watch the rest of the movie with his dick clamped.

On another occasion, Harry sat alone in his dark, cold, parked car, across the street, shivering while shooting a telephoto video of them in a restaurant. Probably toasting to the demise of Harry Waldheim, he thought. The lights were low as the appetizers were served. Harry saw Lippy whisper something across the table, then Georgia burst out in laughter. "Do it now!" he reads her lips ordering Lippy. They were sitting in the front, in full display behind a large plate glass window, when he saw her reach under the table. Judging by the squirming, wide eyed Lipschitz, Harry assumed that a pecker and possibly balls were being secretly tortured. He could just see beads of sweat gathering over Lipschitz's upper lip, but he was not overtly responding to whatever she was doing. He continued to eat his grass-fed black angus smothered with shaved fennel and pomegranate. Two hours, and a hot shower later, Harry was home. He jumped back on line to read Georgia's latest love letter:

When you get up in the morning, after you shower, you need to put on my underwear and wear it all day. When you get back to the hotel room, I want you to put the pins on your dick and on your balls and wear them as long as you can. If you do something for business then wear as much as you can stand or keep my underwear on and wear a pin on each nipple. I'll think more about these instructions so they are clear.

Chapter 31

As she entered Grand Central Station, Georgia chirped into the phone, leaving a message. "Hi! It's me." Her voice was overly friendly, a little too casual and obsequious. "I'm at the gym and then I'll be doing errands all day. Very busy. If you need me just leave a message. I'll see you tonight at 5:30, let's eat in." It was an attempt at a tease. She was following Lipschitz's instructions on how to drive Harry crazy—as well as implying that he should prepare something for dinner.

Harry listened and didn't believe a word. "Everything that goes through her brain and comes out her mouth is a lie," he thought. He translated her message in his mind. "She is very busy and is doing errands today" meant she was out somewhere fucking Lipschitz like there was no tomorrow! Wandering over to his computer, he checked her emails.

From: gomez@optonline.com
To: g.nabokov@gmail.com
Subject: Conference Opportunity

Meet me at the Stamford train station at 11:00 this morning. I booked a room. I'll bring the toys.

From: g.nabokov@gmail.com

To: gomez@optonline.com
Subject: Conference Opportunity

Great!! Harry's out of the picture for the day. He thinks I'm at the gym and doing errands all day and that I'll be spending the night with him, but no worries, I'm just pulling his chain as you instructed. You are my slave and I am your master. See you soon!!! Can't wait!!

Once inside Grand Central, Georgia texted Lipshitz, letting him know she was on her way.

"Gomez...my little pot-bellied piggy...I hope you have some new toys for us...just jumping on the 9:50 express to Stamford...see you soon!!"

Just the thought of this tryst made her extremely horny. Once on the train, she sighed and sank into her seat. She slipped her hand under the coat on her lap and into her pants and slowly began massaging her clitoris while thoughts of her *slave* passed through her head. She idly gazed out the window, at the passing scenery, almost reaching orgasm, pushing herself almost to the brink, but decided to save the real thing for him. For her it was always more intense that way.

Richard Lipschitz was home alone. The wife was working and the kids were at school. He looked into the bathroom mirror, adjusted his toupee, and brushed his giant, fake teeth. He admired himself, looking neat as a pin in business casual—sort of like a golf pro. He winked and grabbed the keys to the leased, silver Lexus.

He sped toward the train station, the consummate player, always studying the "game." He listened to his hero, Nigel Stern, on the CD player, giving him more insight and info into how to pick up women. His dick was hard as a rock.

"If you are going to succeed as a pickup artist, dear friend, you are going to need a bag of tricks. Mine consists of breath mints, condoms, a pen or pencil and a small writing pad. The most important prop, however, is a piece of dryer

lint. Here's what you do. Find the most beautiful woman in the room. Walk up to her without saying a word while holding the lint, then pretend that you've just removed it from her clothing. "Has this been here all evening?" you ask. Then open your palm with the lint in it. You will have just performed a "neg." She should now be somewhat unsettled and you will have gained her attention. Congratulations."

Lipschitz arrived at the station well in advance of Georgia. He took a blue oval pill out of a vial and threw it down with a swig of bottled water and then popped two Chiclets into his gaping maw. In a half hour, they would be fucking like two crazed dogs in the hotel room. The Viagra would keep him hard for several hours. He opened the gym bag, in the passenger seat, and perused the contents: one ball gag, one cock ring, one leather mask, one butt plug, two nipple clips, one leather harness, a dog collar, and finally a giant, horse-choking, black rubber cock.

"Oh, fuck. Where's the electric dildo?" He frantically pawed through the gym bag. "Oh, there you are," he cooed. He'd forgotten that he bought it especially for Georgia and had it gift wrapped in a different bag. Everything was ready. Another perfect fuck was on the way.

"Last stop. Stamford, Connecticut," droned the conductor. The doors slid open on Georgia's train.

Georgia snapped to, straightened her signature black stretch pants, and threw down the last few drops of vodka from her silver flask (a gift from Richard) and tossed it into her canvas satchel. She eyed the recently purchased tube of KY jelly—her contribution to the afternoon.

"Why is she always the last one out of the train?" Lipschitz wondered aloud. His pulse quickened as he finally spotted his dominatrix-in-training ambling toward the parking lot. "Over here," he called out, waving and holding the passenger door open. She flopped in, pretending to ignore him as he handed her his recently-filled matching Tiffany silver flask.

Georgia took a swig of the vodka, which burned and numbed at the same time. "Let's get it on, big boy. Time's-a-wasting."

Taking her cue, Richard floored it, pretending to be a Nascar driver for the two-block journey to the Holiday Inn.

Georgia put down her bag and went directly to the shower, ordering Richard to strip down, over her shoulder, before closing the door. Once in his black, boner-dominated speedos, partially obscured by an overhanging, recently waxed gut, he laid out the contents of his gym bag, imagining himself to be a curator at the Museum of Sex. How clever he was, he thought, attending to every detail so perfectly.

"I hope you brought the lube dear," he chirped as Georgia emerged, steam billowing from the open bathroom door, her head wrapped in a towel. She was naked which showed off her recent Brazilian wax job. Her hands were cupped in offering, and proffered the soon-to-be-opened, and soon-to-be-depleted, tube of KY.

"Now take this gift and get ready to *make some L-O-V-E*, bitch," she ordered, eyeing the assortment of toys so painstakingly laid out for her perusal.

Eight and a half hours later, Georgia was headed back into the city on the train. Her cheeks were bright red from Lipschitz's abrasive beard. Her eyes were glazed from the dopamine surge and endorphins. She had lost count of all the orgasms. She was on the phone with Harry, two hours after her proposed meeting time. It was 7:30 and the dinner he carefully prepared was cold and sad.

"Hi Harry, I'm running a little late."

He heard the sound of the train doors closing and the high-pitched tones specific to Metro North Railroad.

"You're on a train..."

"Yeah, I'm on the number 6 train," she lied.

"How can you call from the subway?" he asked, knowing full well where she was.

"Oh yeah, you can do that now from the number 6," she said.

"Lying bitch," he muttered, slightly under his breath.

"What did you say?" she asked, though she heard him well enough.

"I said, I'll see you soon dear."

Harry wasn't at all surprised. He knew that she and Lipschitz were plotting to drive him crazy. He knew that she was only pretending to want him as a lover. She was always coming up with excuses, like *I need time and space to be alone. You are my best friend Harry. I'm so conflicted about my feelings toward everybody. I don't think I love Richard, but the poor guy needs me.*

Harry read every single email; it had been months, yet he continued to play along. He was hooked on the game, as crazy as it was, and as addicted as they both were. In spite of how much it hurt to read all the details of when they met and what they did to each other, he continued—a masochist feeding on their sadism.

Chapter 32

Harry Waldheim's journal

Not because they are particularly in love or even like each other very much; rather, the triangle feeds them, keeping them alive, filling them with life forces like no other: hatred, anger, and self-loathing.

Chapter 33

Harry and Georgia were together for almost eight years, and not once did he actually feel like he was "in love" with her. But now with all of this diversion, this scheming sport, he wondered if he was actually falling in love with her. Deep down, he knew it was about the game over anything else.

They both knew they were just pretending to follow the instructions of Doctor Gladstone (and for Georgia, the added instructions of Lipschitz: *"Fuck this guy's brain. Drive him crazy. And, most importantly, keep him the fuck away from me and my family!"*). Harry played along, partly just to see where this game would go. He wondered how the plot would thicken and began to feel strangely more a connected part of this *manage a trios*.

"So Georgia," he kissed her softly on the neck, and she let him. This slight softening of her guard pulled Harry closer and he pondered ripping her clothes off and running his hands all over her naked body—licking every molecule and follicle. "You said I haven't acknowledged you. I am sorry if I did that," he lied.

"Thank you," she lied.

"Do you think it's a pattern with us? You feeling unheard, and feeling abandoned?" Harry asked, feigning sensitivity.

"Always. And maybe. I am confused," she replied, already uncomfortable doing this stupid exercise.

"It's understandable. Me too," Harry said.

"I'm just fucked up. But you are my best friend, Harry."

She put her arms around Harry and he drew her to him, hugging her tight.

"Really? So why are you doing this thing—this awful thing with this disgusting guy?"

"Don't say that. It's not like that." Georgia pulled away as her phone chirped out the dreaded electronic version of Mozart's Piano Concerto #16 in C major.

"Georgia, please don't answer that."

"I have to."

She disappeared into the bathroom with the phone. Harry heard her muffled voice saying, "I'll call you back in fifteen minutes. Yeah, I'm just getting rid of him now."

Georgia sat on the toilet seat, lid closed and sent the following text to Richard:

> *When you get up in the morning, after you shower, you need to put on my underwear and wear it all day. When you get back to the hotel room, I want you to keep my underwear on and wear tight clips on each nipple. I'll think more about these instructions so they are clear.*

Georgia left the bathroom and walked over to Harry, lying on the couch, looking up at the ceiling. He sat up and they distantly embraced. Nothing was said. It was enough for one day, she thought. She was only here to do her job, distract Harry and try to protect Lipschitz. It was, after all, the dominant's obligation to insure the safety of her submissive. She had convinced her beloved Richard that Harry was a frightening and dangerous psychopath and now could be in control of both men.

Chapter 34

A week after what Harry hoped would be a so-called mirroring session: a reunion, an understanding, a meeting of the minds and maybe even a seduction, they returned to the home office of Doctor Gladstone. It was plain to him Georgia's motive was to confuse Harry and keep him away from her beloved Lipschitz. She also wanted to keep the meeting at the therapist's as brief as possible.

"So, tell me what's happening between you two."

Harry looked at Georgia with genuine hope, but secretly pressed the record button on the device hidden in his pocket. His archive was growing daily.

The farther away she got, the more Harry wanted her back. And so he began to treat the couple's therapy sessions with a bit more enthusiasm. He bubbled forth, "Well, I think we're beginning to communicate in a way that we never did in the past. I realized that I often took Georgia's criticism of me as a reprimand, like when I was a little boy and would withdraw. I hoped I had evolved beyond that, but..."

"Okay, if I may interrupt?" Doctor Gladstone asked. "Everybody has parts of them that are immature. We go through certain traumas as we are growing up, and inside, there are parts of us that get frozen in time. Now, I just want to show you a diagram about parts being frozen." He began to draw a diagram of stick figures on a white flip chart page. The smell of the Magic Marker filled the small space.

"Now let's say that Georgia represents the moment of the most extreme trauma, when the pain is at its height. Remember what it was like to be young? Like when kids hold their breath to stop something from happening. Well, we know that doesn't work, but it does serve to freeze the experience, when we are approaching the moment of the greatest pain. The unconscious recognizes this and tries to stop it right here." He drew a dotted line, with an arrow point, and rested the marker there. Like, if we don't stop it here, we are not going to survive."

Harry nodded, paying close attention.

Georgia had completely checked out and was remembering escapades with Lipschitz. They were in a hotel parking lot in Scottsdale, Arizona. Lipschitz had rented a black SUV and made the back into a bed using white sheets, pillows and blankets from the hotel they were staying in. A silver champagne bucket filled with ice and a bottle of bubbly sat on the open tailgate. Lipschitz, dressed in his usual golf pro outfit, held two champagne glasses as Georgia approached, giggling at this silly scene. She snapped photographs as they toasted each other.

Gladstone took a brief breath, noticed both responses, then continued.

"When in reality the pain here," he circled the drawing for emphasis, "is not all that different from the pain you are feeling right now. But you don't know that. So, this part, the abused child, gets frozen in time and holds the pain, while the rest of the self continues to evolve. Some people have many parts in this condition and are quite disassociated. The part that took the abuse, held it and didn't evolve, when something similar occurs, be it a voice, tone, or whatever, triggers the frozen abuse response. So, instead of being the age you are, you regress. You may have evolved mostly as an adult, but the abused, frozen parts have remained frozen in time and are activated by triggers."

Doctor Gladstone took a hefty swig from his stainless steel coffee mug. "Let me congratulate you both on working on those communication exercises."

Georgia awakened, "We only did it twice."

"It's so new. I hope we can do this every day," Harry said, looking to Georgia for a response.

She looked at the floor and exhaled with an exasperated sigh.

"Georgia, are you still with us?" asked the doctor, knowing full well that she wasn't.

"What? Oh yeah, of course, but I think I need a time out from Harry."

"So, now you're thinking that maybe the best way to deal with the problems in your relationship is to take time off to work things through? Is that what you're saying?

"Yes."

Why do you think that would be a better choice, now that the two of you are acknowledging that there are issues and working on those? I'm curious what your thinking is on that, Georgia," Doctor Gladstone said objectively.

After a long pause, Georgia tried a response. "Well, I think it's important to identify and.....ummmmm analyze the problems. And maybe there are things that I'm not aware of...you know, it goes both ways. And it's really valuable to examine what those things are, no matter what happens. And so by separation... I don't know what I mean by separation... Before my relationship with Richard, you know my relationship that I have with Richard..." She trailed off for a moment and then continued her ramble.

"But I suppose that's really, really, really important, but... I don't want that issue..." she trailed off again, lost in a cloud of ideas that she couldn't seem to make come together.

"It's unfair of me to say," making another valiant attempt to get her true point across without making it sound like she was steering her agenda, "but it's hard to get around. To me it seems that there's so much stuff that preceded my—this affair. I need time and space." She folded her hands in her lap and nodded, satisfactorily, a slight smile crossing her otherwise vacant expression.

There it was. Her mantra. Time and space, Harry thought.

"So, I am clearly in limbo here." His voice was thin with anxiety. He was genuinely afraid of being abandoned, even if it meant no more contact with his torturers. They, at least, provided some connection...but connection with what, he wondered.

"That's true. It's a very, very difficult position to be in." Gladstone's sympathies were with Harry as he stared at Georgia.

"Well, I've already lost at least twenty pounds in the last month ...I'll probably lose another hundred before this is over. I am totally out to sea here. I am abjectly alone. I need human contact. Life is so not fair." Harry's voice thinned even more. "Fuck me..."

"Get a dog." Georgia lobbed, snapping back into the session.

"Screw you," whispered Harry, under his breath.

"You're feeling sorry for yourself," Gladstone interjected, like the couples therapist he was.

"I *am* feeling sorry for myself," Harry moaned, "I didn't do this. I was put into this position. I have a right to feel sorry for myself." Harry's breathing became increasingly uneven, with all the cortisol blasting through his system. He felt faint.

"Well, actually, you don't." This bit of tough love from Gladstone came as a surprise.

"Well, I beg to differ with you."

"This will not serve you. It will totally hurt you," stated Gladstone, softening slightly.

"Okay then, what am I supposed to do?"

Gladstone got down to business.

"First you have to hammer out a separation. And then you have to make some decisions about what you are going to do with this time. You are in a tremendous amount of pain and are doing everything you can to hang on to Georgia. The more you hold on, the more you will be pushing her away. It's sort of like the little kid who gets spanked by a parent and then goes back to that same parent for comfort."

This guy was so fucking right, Harry thought. "That was exactly how I grew up, so..."

"That's the pattern we need to break. You need to learn to comfort yourself. It's been my experience that the greatest healing comes from self-love." Gladstone looked at the two of them, knowing full well that they didn't have a snowball's chance in hell at reconciliation.

Before they left, they agreed to meet at Harry's loft for one more fake mirroring session. After that, Georgia proposed they not see each other for a month.

Fine, thought Harry. *You might not see me. But I'll see you.*

Heading toward the 96th Street subway station, they walked in silence, neither wanting to discuss the uncomfortable therapy session, or anything at all, really. Georgia dreamt of being back in the arms of Lipshitz and Harry reflected on his childhood again.

Chapter 35

He was one of the smallest boys in his fourth grade class, but what he lacked in size was compensated for with a tough, stubborn resolve and a temper that made even his largest adversaries think twice about messing with him. Not that he looked for trouble, but it always seemed to come his way. He never backed down and never took shit from anybody and the day he came close to getting killed was no exception.

Harry and his friend, Dave Wheeler, had stayed after school an extra two hours to help their teacher, Mrs. Crand, prepare for the weekly puppet show. They spent the time cleaning the stage, putting a final coat of paint on several of the main characters, and making sure everything was perfect.

It was a warm spring afternoon as they unlocked their bikes from the rack next to The Presley School, as Tommy Mudgett, Chuck Prentis and Butch Walker, three flunkies from the retard class who were a good bit bigger and older because they'd been held back a grade or two, toughs from "the other side of the tracks" approached.

"Fuck you Squire," yelled Prentis to Harry, making fun of his Viking haircut. Doug Wheeler quickly mounted his bike and bolted, leaving Harry alone to fend for himself. Adrenalin coursed through Harry's veins, though he said nothing. He slowly removed the lock from his bike and clipped it to the seat. "Who's gonna protect you now Squire...looks like your little boyfriend ran away," taunted the tallest flunky as they circled closer, like a pack of hyenas. Harry, assessed the situation. It was three against one and Wheeler was probably already home, hiding under his bed.

Mudgett, Prentis and Walker edged closer, cutting Harry off from any chance of escape, three predators were cutting a weakling from the herd. Very slowly, as if in slow motion he glanced down at his watch; it was 4:30. He thought about his mother at home, preparing dinner; his brother watching cartoons on channel 6. He remembered two days ago, the Walker's two feral Rottweilers got loose and nearly tore the neighbor's beagle in half. He'd never seen so much blood, ever. It was amazing that the beagle survived. Now he always carried a club made of solid maple to protect himself from not only the Rottweilers but several of the other vicious dogs his neighbors felt should be allowed to run free. It was a shame he didn't have it with him now, but he wasn't allowed to bring it to school and the principal confiscated it when he did.

Then suddenly—BLAM... A punch to Harry's jaw snapped him out of his daydream. Hot, numb, flushed skin felt no pain, just warmth—the heat of blood rushing to the sight of an injury. This sensation was not new for him; between his father slamming him around and numerous encounters with bullies in his school, this was familiar territory. Harry could take a beating.

He threw his bike down in the sand and the toughs backed up slightly. "Fuck all of you!" screamed Harry, and he charged into the nearest body, wrestling him to the ground. Prentis and Walker grabbed Harry by the arms and pulled him off a screaming Mudgett, who picked himself up and laughed as he, slammed Harry in the face with a closed fist before wildly pummeling his stomach.

Harry managed to squirm away from Walker and Prentis, at the same time tripping Mudgett by hooking his right foot behind an ankle and slamming Mudgett's knee with his left foot, sending him crashing in pain to the ground. Once free of his captors on either side and the third guy on the ground, it was only two against one, at least for a while. Harry considered his options: stay and fight or beat a hasty retreat into the woods, his true home and sanctuary.

"Ooohh...does somebody want to fight?" taunted Walker, getting excited. Harry backed away, toward the woods and was just about to turn and run when, behind him, the two older brothers of Prentis and Walker appeared.

"Where are you going dipshit?" one of them asked, blocking Harry's escape. "You have a fight to finish." The elder Prentis, shoved him toward the young savages. Encouraged by their older siblings, the boys begin slapping, punching, spitting and kicking.

The odds against Harry only strengthened his resolve. Time came almost to a standstill; in his mind, combat slowed down to a single frame at a time, he felt no pain and his world quieted.

He did all that he could possibly do, as outnumbered as he was: singling out an individual, grasping throats, head butting and punching faces, only to be dragged off by the other two. The older brothers egged them on like fans at a cock fight. Mudgett squirmed out of Harry's strangle hold, aided by his two friends, and as he crawled away, he discovered a baseball bat. It had probably been lying in the tall grass between The Presley School and the woods for a few years. It was gray with age and broken in half, only the fatter, business end remaining.

Up to that point, the battle seemed almost a stalemate. Harry fought back fiercely, fearlessly, a lunatic warrior, when suddenly he began to feel the sharp blows of the bat, as it hit his back, shoulders and arms. He could hear the older brothers barking, "Hit him in the head...hit him in the head." But by some miracle this order was never obeyed, or the younger boys lacked the skills required to actually hit him in the head.

Harry, hearing that taunt, squirmed away from the mauling Prentis and Walker and faced Mudgett, who kept slamming Harry repeatedly, with the bat, hitting the same mark on his upper left arm, over and over. Harry charged Mudgett like an angry, bloodied bull, blindly, with nothing left to lose, and wrestled the bat away, swinging insanely at all three adversaries who circled him at a safe distance, afraid of getting hit. Harry lunged toward Prentis who fell over backward. Instantly, Harry was on top of him, poised to slam him in the face with the bat, when something snapped. He couldn't bring himself to hit this kid...not with a bat, anyway. Some force stronger than his instinct to survive—or for revenge—stopped him in his tracks. In that moment time stopped, for everyone. Walker and Mudgett stood back, the older brothers shut up, and Prentis froze, expecting to be dead, or at least out cold, missing most of his teeth. Harry, breathing harder than he'd ever breathed in all of his ten years, stood up, walked a few feet to the edge of the woods, and hurled the broken bat over the embankment. All was quiet.

Breaking the silence, a hermit thrush sang a few measures of his lonely, solitary song: a virtuosic solo of pan pipes ringing in the peaceful woods, harmonizing with gently rustling leaves and a chorus of late afternoon crickets. The older brothers, with a sideways glance and nod of their heads, signaled the fight was over and that they were disappointed with the younger boys and, in their own silent way, expressed their approval of Harry's kicking ass in a three against one assault. Silently, everyone left the school ground—everyone except Harry, who disoriented and still sucking in daggers of breath, searched for his bicycle and a few books scattered in the sand and crabgrass. His body was beginning to thaw; the numbness dissipating. His left arm throbbed painfully from Mudgett's repeated clobbering with the bat. It was swollen to twice it's normal size and bent in a rather unnatural way. He climbed on his bike, bruised and aching all over, in excruciating pain, fighting back tears, looking in amazement at his disfigured arm as he rode, one handed, toward home.

Chapter 36

The first time Harry looked at Georgia's email, hacking in could not have been simpler. They shared the exact same password. Back, before all this happened, they had no secrets, and nothing to hide. They were, in Harry's estimation, happy together, not insanely in love, mind you, but getting along—coexisting. The second password hack, after he'd been found out, wasn't too difficult either. Lipschitz opened up new email accounts for himself and Georgia, with new passwords. They turned out to be "Georgia" for Lipshitz and "Gomez" for Georgia. It hadn't been too difficult to figure out. Actually, Harry guessed both of them in about sixty seconds, knowing how literal and simple good old Dick was.

The third password, however, threw Harry for a loop. For several days, try as he might, he could not get back in. Following them had become an addiction—his fetish—and not being able to access the emails put a serious damper on what had become his life's work. No amount of guessing worked. Hours of attempting combinations of old passwords, adding numbers and pet's names, middle names, maiden names, favorite wine, on and on—nothing worked. And then it hit him: let her show me her new password. After their appointment with Doctor Gladstone, he began to set the trap.

Harry and Georgia, throughout the turmoil of the past year and their slow-moving breakup, remained connected, although the terms of their agreement were never official or formally agreed upon. Neither of them could completely let go. They saw each other at least once a week, both making excuses like "Could you help me with a chore?" or "I need to borrow something." or "How do you do this or that on your computer using the new software upgrade?" Neither admitting to their thinly disguised fabrications. Sure, she had to protect Lipschitz and Harry was obsessed with spying, but still, their feelings for one another seemed to deepen in ways that neither of them understood. They both loved and despised each other in equal measure. They were, for all intents and purposes, enmeshed adversaries. *Be close to your friends but closer to your enemies,* Harry said to himself, though not completely certain of his motives.

With all the information he gathered, destroying Lipschitz, his family, and any future career, not to mention his relationship with the bondage/discipline/sadomasochist community, would be a simple matter of a few letters, phone calls, and forwarded emails. It would be easy. He could also discredit Georgia to her family and friends. And yet he refrained, knowing that she and Richard Lipschitz would probably self-destruct and reveal themselves to the world all by themselves. Eventually.

Georgia continued to spend time with Harry, teasing him and more. Harry knew she was justifying this "breach of protocol" in her head, but for his part, he enjoyed playing along and teasing her, as well. He became increasingly attracted, aroused, and devious. He started to experiment, to see how far he could go or what would happen. He began by adding small amounts of ground-up propranolol, Ambien, or Klonopin to some of her drinks. Two crushed Ambien tablets mixed with a glass of chardonnay would put her in the mood. A suggestion of a foot massage was never refused, and then Harry would set to work. Moving up her legs with his large, intelligent hands—he'd get most of the way up, toward her well-manicured garden, then pause and tease and patiently retreat. He'd begin massaging a hand, and then move up along her arms, knowingly seeking out the erogenous zones on the backs of her upper triceps. He'd remove her shirt, massaging her back, then kiss her ear, nibbling, working his teeth from her neck, down her arm and to her back before slipping a hand down to unbutton the front of her trousers and sliding the zipper open, work his teeth over her exposed buttocks. His hand would part the tight cloves, a finger sensually scraping over the hot, textured anal pore before moving on to the moist entrance of her warm, prized gash, and then past it, to the rigid nub, which he massaged with utter tenderness and firm, slightly vibrating pressure.

At this point, she was on the verge of passing out, yet so close to orgasm. Harry could, and would, continue this tease for hours until, precisely at 9:30 p.m., the cheesy electronic Mozart interrupted and she disappeared into the bathroom for a half hour. Then she'd straighten her clothes and leave for home. During every such encounter, Harry's various recording devices whirred away, capturing these historic moments for the archive. The aphrodisiac of sneaking, spying, and deceiving, would be in full-tilt for them both, owing to the games each played.

Two weeks after their latest therapy appointment, Georgia arrived for their final get-together before the thirty-day separation.

"Hey there. Before I do anything, mind if I check my e-mail?" Georgia sat at the computer and typed in her password as the hidden camera above captured every keystroke. She read several neurotic messages from Lipschitz, who knew that she was visiting Harry. One of the emails provided a series of suggestions on how to act during the meeting:

1) No hugging or kissing; only a handshake.

2) Speak unemotionally and be distant

3) If he gets emotional, suggest that you leave immediately.

4) Make sure that in no uncertain terms is he to have any contact with you for the next 30 days. This includes any e-mail, snail mail, phone calls or personal visits, whatsoever!

5) As soon as you leave, meet me at 1011 Park Avenue. I will be waiting with a bottle of your favorite white and my favorite red, a new toy for us, and two fleet enemas [not optional]. I will be hiding under the covers on my knees with my ass in the air, waiting for your whip and further instructions. YBF

They did a very short mirroring exercise, with Georgia only going through the motions, and following the instructions of Lipschitz to the letter. She kept her distance while Harry, pathetically, actually tried being sincere. He tried to win her back with apologies, understanding, kindness, and, yes, manipulation, even though he was also making a secret audio recording of their session, and everything else on their last day. He knew he wouldn't see her for a month and would certainly miss the depraved, drug induced sex.

"No time for a last glass of Chardonnay, dear? How about one last foot massage? I'll miss you."

Georgia left as quickly as possible, with only a nod.

Once she was gone, Harry played back the recording he'd just made.

"Well, I've...we've both...had some time, and I think that it is best for both of us to take some kind of separation. And I guess that involves some kind of ground rules," she said, obeying her submissive love slave to the letter.

"Did you say ground rules?" Harry heard himself ask.

"Yes. I think that we need to have a thirty day period of zero communication, um, whatsoever. And to leave our options open. You know, to see other people. I just think it's for the best. But I will still be happy to stop by while you are in California to water your plants. I still have your key."

"So, what you're saying is that you want me to leave you and your boyfriend alone. But you're okay with watering my plants while I'm away, attempting to recover from the most traumatic event of my life—you leaving me. And you think it's okay to have *my* key," whined Harry.

He could hear how pathetic and self-pitying he sounded, but it didn't matter. It was all part of the game.

Exasperated with his sarcasm, she responded, "What I meant about other people is that anything could happen. You know, I might have to travel for work and be away for a year. Or, I could get very sick, or, I can't predict the future. But, I think this will be good for both of us."

She paused for a moment as Harry attempted to regroup. Then, continued, saying, "I think that a lot of what's going on is in your head. You've got this movie playing, and it's not real."

"Can you please stop now?" Harry cut her off. "I have to respond to that. This movie in my head, this fiction, has only to do with your relationship with Richard Lipschitz, and my reading of the forty pages of e-mails between the two of you, seeing his picture, and then finally meeting this so-called *man*, knowing what kind of person he is."

He could see that Georgia was tuned out, drifting off into who knew where, although he could guess. Definitely far away from him and his anger.

He continued, "Seeing how he dresses, how he combs his glued on hair, imagining him jerking off on your face, cumming in your asshole, sliming all over you. And you loving every minute of it, and, god knows, doing whatever else back to him. Falling in love. Tying each other up in little knots, ball gagging, being in a constant state of sexual ecstasy with this man who is *a real person*, not a movie in my head. Who has a wife and three children and is a whore-mongering, rich, fat cat. Who is, in my mind, taking advantage of a vulnerable, extremely attractive woman with exceptionally low self-esteem. And using her as his personal seminal receptacle."

"Okay... May I go now?" Georgia asked.

He realized, as he listened to the playback, that she had not heard a second of the diatribe.

"Sure," responded Harry. Just as well, he thought, I really laid into her. It's more important to the project that she return here during the month I'm away, hopefully with the boyfriend.

They exchanged ice-cold hugs and superficial pecks on cheeks, and with a final nod, she was gone. The door closed without ceremony or drama. It was done; a new chapter.

Harry locked it behind her, grabbed the step ladder, ejected the camera card, and popped it into his editing system. Her hands appeared, perfectly in focus, typing with great care and precision: n-a-b-o-k-o-v. Exuberant, Harry could hack, follow and spy, once again. The camera recorded everything perfectly and Harry was again able to access her e-mail with the new password. Nabokov—I should have known..." grumbled Harry, "after all that Russian princess bullshit..."

Anticipating Georgia would bring her beloved Richard to help with the plant watering, Harry set up several hidden, motion-activated video surveillance cameras, disguised as smoke detectors: one in the bedroom, one in the bathroom, one in the kitchen, and one over the couch.

Sure enough, the very same day he left for California, for his month of "time and space," they popped over. The hidden video cameras activated as Georgia and Lipschitz explored the loft—and one another. They went to his loft almost every day he was away. It seemed the thrill of violating his space made for hotter sex. Lipschitz brought over some bondage magazines from his collection to show Georgia. They read them together on the couch as they groped one another. Carelessly, or perhaps not, they left them behind for Harry to find on his return.

Chapter 37

Meanwhile, in California, Harry tended to his wounds, plotted his next moves, and tried to gain the approval of his dear friend and guru, Alex Forsythe, brilliant, alopecian former movie director. Alex lived in L.A., where he wrote screenplays and conducted production meetings—mostly pretending to work, as his past was filled with blockbuster cult hits for which he received massive residual payments. Work? Who needs it. He had an off-the-charts IQ and was an avid student of human nature. An eccentric himself, he had been collecting freaks his entire life, and found Harry's situation one of the more fascinating he had witnessed in years. He invited Harry to visit during his "separation" period, to recoup and regroup. He met Harry at the airport and they drove to his home in Venice, talking and gossiping all the way.

"I need you to help me," Harry said, the second he slid into the passenger seat.

Alex already knew part of the story—enough to glean that Harry might be asking him to take part in some kind of revenge scheme. "Look, I get what's going on, but I'm an adulterer myself, and it might come back to bite me karmically if I help you,"

"So what...I need your help. It's not you who's fucking around on me. This is about friendship."

"Thank you. I just needed an adjustment," responded Alex, cynically, and drove on. His small white poodle sat in his lap with its brown-stained muzzle nestled in Alex's left hand, his cell phone rang and Alex answered it with his right hand. Now he was driving no-handed. He was always multi-tasking and distracted, always on the brink of some catastrophe yet, somehow, he always walked away unscathed.

While Alex was on the phone, Harry drifted off, barely seeing the tired, single story structures lining Lincoln Avenue, on their way to Venice. He found himself half-daydreaming about the time he found out Georgia and Lipschitz were planning a trip to Austria.

He had run into Georgia, on the track, at Chelsea Piers Gym. As they walked together, making small talk, Georgia said, "I'm taking a little trip next week."

"Oh, where to?"

"Austria."

"Austria?"

"With Richard."

"Oh....fine....and how are you going to pay for this?"

Harry was shocked, his ears were burning as he silently walked a few feet ahead of Georgia, as if to get away from her. Suddenly, he turned around, yelling louder than he had ever yelled in his life. "Lipschitz is a dead man. I will cut him from ear to ear. I will rip out his heart and shove it down his throat. I will chew all the skin off his face. I will destroy him and his family!"

"Harry...calm down.." She said, with more than a touch of fear in her voice. After all, she'd never seen him in this kind of state. She followed him as he ranted, walking around the track, in full public view, talking trash. "Harry...please..."

Harry, screaming for a good 15 minutes, finally made it to the bleachers with Georgia in tow, pleading with him to lower his voice and calm down. They sat, Harry taking long deep breaths. His face was beet red and he shook but no one seemed to hear or pay any attention to his loud display of rage as hundreds of well-toned gym rats pumped iron and developed their cores on countless treadmills, buried in headphones blasting upbeat motivational workout tunes.

"OK...I'm not going. I've changed my mind, I'm staying," she said.

Lying cunt, thought Harry.

By the time they arrived at Alex's house, Harry filled in the details of that day. They remained in the car, talking.

"So then I tell her to get on the phone and call Lipschitz and tell him right then and there that the trip is canceled. Which she does. Of course, next thing I find out that they *did* go on this trip."

"How did you find out?" Alex asked.

Harry could see that Alex was fascinated by the story, but he knew how Alex's mind worked and could tell there was a movie idea, unfolding before his eyes. He wondered, briefly, when Alex would start on the screenplay?

"I called Lipschitz's wife."

"Oh my god. You talked to his wife."

"I called his wife, and I said, 'this is Stephen Katz,' and I gave her a phone number (coincidentally, of a defunct S&M dungeon). I asked if Dick was around. And she said no, he wasn't and I asked, 'Oh, did he go off to Austria?' And she said, 'Yeah, he's in Austria.'"

"Wow," Alex smiled, "you gave her the number of the S&M club?"

"Yeah."

"You monster."

Alex considered for a moment, and then said, "You know, there's always the possibility that Lipschitz could have you killed."

"Who cares?" Harry tossed it off. "If I'm dead I'm dead."

They got out, unloaded Harry's bag from the car, and headed into the compound. The place was a sanctuary for freaks who rented several shacks within the conglomeration of plants, chickens, cats, dogs, defunct furniture, and the remnants of too many unfinished projects.

Soon they found themselves in the garden, sitting on what was left of two wooden Adirondack chairs.

"I think I may have talked her into giving me a session; you know...tied up, whipped, gagged, bound and all that. Actually tricked her into it," Harry said, with a degree of pride.

The garden was walled-in, haphazardly maintained, and mostly overgrown. Several chickens scratched around, kicking up dust in the background.

"So you mean to tell me that you're having an affair with your ex-girlfriend behind the back of the guy she left you for? And he's in love with her."

"He's totally in love with her." Harry paused, examining the chaos of his surroundings. "I *am* going to kill him, eventually."

"Oh my god. I love it when you say stuff like that. Now *that* turns me on. I wish I had a tape recording of this!"

"I *am* recording this."

"You're recording this as we speak?"

"Yeah, I record everything."

"Outrageous. 'I am going to kill him eventually.' No actor could ever say it as perfectly as you just said it." Alex shifted into director-mode second gear. as two of his dirt bag, stoner, hippie tenants skulked by in the background. "Wow Harry, I'm impressed. I'm excited. We're going to make this into a movie!"

"I guess I should do something with the hundreds of hours of secretly taped conversations, most of which I've transcribed. And did I tell you I have over two thousand printed out e-mails, and countless hours of home porn? Why should we let this all go to waste?"

"Plus, you're living in your own movie. This is going to be a docudrama, not a mocudrama. A real guy's life is going to be destroyed here. This is more than revenge...this is therapy, man!"

They fell into silence as Harry surveyed the garden. Two dogs yipped frantically at a hissing cat, crouched beneath a tired wooden deck. Several other cats clustered on a picnic table, eating leftover people food, while one snoozed on top of the chips in a large bowl. Animals, Harry thought—a house full of animals. This house is clearly dominated by animals.

Chapter 38

When Harry returned from his month in California, not only were his plants watered, but his surveillance recorders were filled with much more than he could have ever imagined. Not bothering to unpack, he got right down to the business of dumping all the new sound and video data into his editing system. He watched with both horror and amazement, pain and pleasure. He sat at his computer, staring at every image, every grainy surveillance frame, picking up tidbits of audio at fifteen frames per second. The movement was choppy, but it was way more than enough information.

The footage was shot from motion sensitive, miniature cameras, hidden in fake smoke detectors mounted on the ceiling. Like the rough video, the audio lacked perfection, but was completely understandable. Not only could Harry see them, but he could listen to everything they said, on camera or off.

Georgia entered the apartment, pulling the reluctant and paranoid Lipschitz through the door, she bellowed, "Helloooo," to show Lippy the apartment was really empty. He had been concerned Harry was still there and the whole thing might have been a trap.

"Georgia, are you sure the psycho isn't here waiting for us with a hatchet?" Harry heard Lipschitz ask.

But there was no sign of Harry, the coast was clear and he was three thousand miles away, as promised. The overhead camera in the kitchen revealed Georgia opening two bottles of wine: white for her and red for him. They sat at the table, poured the wine, and toasted, professing their love for each other.

They drank, chatting about nothing. All the while, Lipschitz surveyed Harry's apartment like a homicide detective. "Strange place," he declared, noting the contents. The living area of Harry's apartment held tons of books, a few obscure plants, eclectic pieces of assorted modern and antique furniture, several computers, and a wide variety of paintings and small sculptures. Most of the art was from Harry's past life as a polystylist and included everything from photorealism to abstract expressionism. It was a large, once mostly open, loft space now crammed with stuff, which impressed and intimidated and aroused Lipschitz's suspicions. *How could this eccentric crackpot possibly afford such a luxury space?*

"What does this guy do, again?" he asked, already with two glasses of red wine under his belt. He looked Georgia in the eye, briefly, then continued his surveillance of the space.

"He does a little bit of everything. Sort of a creative producer type, and he has a dead, rich uncle who was some kind of German industrialist. But who cares about him? How about a tour of the loft, my little Gomez?" Georgia lead him to the living area, his back to the couch. "Now have a seat," she shoved him down forcefully.

"Don't hurt me," he said, hands up in mock supplication as his pudgy rear end slammed into the cushion, "I'll do whatever you want." His trouser trout was already hard as a rock.

"Shut up and take off your cloths," she commanded.

He obeyed, quickly removing everything except his black speedos, his bulging pecker wanting out.

"Those too," she said, pointing to the speedos.

He obeyed, immediately placing his last garment atop a neat pile on the floor.

"And what shall I do with these?" she asked, cupping his balls tenderly in her hands. She removed clothespins from her handbag, pinning them carefully to his scrotum, stretching the loose, hairless, waxed skin as he writhed with pain and pleasure. While on her knees facing him, she pretended to ignore the bobbing cock in her face. She continued to fasten clothespins onto his flabby abdomen as Dick's hard pecker swayed and waved, gently grazing the side of her face and hair.

"Now," she pronounced, having added about a dozen clothespins, "we're going to have to do something about *this*." She held his hard-on in both hands, like a hairless puppy, caressing its sides with her thumbs as though it had soft, leather ears. She looked at the engorged head with its tiny vertical smile. "Now what do *you* want?" she asked in baby talk. "Woodgy-woodgy-woodgy." She gave it a teasing kiss, rubbed it on her face, and then licked it, before pulling a short length of climbing rope from her bag.

"How about this?" She began tying slip knots up its very average length.

Harry watched as Lipschitz's breath deepened.

"Oh, let's see now." She pulled a black leather, zippered falcon hood, complete with traces and bells, made specially for Richard, from her satchel. "No ball gag today," laughed Georgia, "I'm putting your tongue to work very soon."

"Yes mistress," breathed an obviously excited Lipschitz.

Georgia quickly removed her clothes, scattering them haphazardly around the room, and stood defiantly in front of him. Richard couldn't see her but Harry sure could. Naked, silent, a glass of Chardonnay in one hand, a cigarette in the other, she ever so slowly moved closer and closer, blowing smoke toward his face. He squirmed as a final blast of smoke flowed into the unzipped nose and mouth openings of the hood. She downed the remainder of the Chardonnay, put the cigarette butt in the glass, and spun around with her back to him. Bent over, with her naked, open ass in his face, she commanded, "Now get to work and rim me, you bitch!"

Even though he couldn't hear everything clearly or make out all the particulars, Harry had seen enough for a while and put the editing system to sleep. He got up and walked over to the couch, the exact same spot he just saw being defiled in the video. Shaking his head, he pretended to be pushed backward, falling to the spot where Georgia shoved Lipschitz. He threw his head back and opened his arms wide, absent-mindedly running his hands under the cushion. His fingertips found a stack of magazines. Harry stood and pulled the cushions out to find about a dozen or so: *Domination Directory International, Fetish Times, Ritual, Marquis, Skin Two, Prometheus, Rage,* and so on. He opened up a *Marquis*. It seemed to be mostly devoted to latex and vinyl, with photographs of men and women of all shapes and sizes wearing black and blue rubbery corsets, masks, hoods, ass exposing chaps, hot pants, gas masks, gauntlet cuffs, boots, dildo belts. They were bound, gagged, pierced, suspended, collared, cuffed, and filleted like fish.

Harry sat back down, motionless, on the defiled couch. "I've struck gold," he said, and smiled, pleased with his surveillance and the stack of just discovered magazines. He started to shake, adrenalin pumping, in fight or flight mode. The feeling was a familiar and perversely comfortable home.

Chapter 39

Later that afternoon, Harry picked up the phone to share his news. "Oh man, Liv, you wouldn't believe it. They used my apartment, they used my bed." Harry spoke in an excited staccato.

"Ohhhh, your bed. Throw it away. Throw it away, Harry. I mean it. It's cursed. Plus, it's disgusting!"

Harry couldn't let her finish her thought, and didn't even register her concern for his mental state before continuing. "And they left their trash magazines under my fucking couch."

"Gross. But why?"

"Who the fuck knows? Guess the whole experience made everything hotter. Knowing they were *doing it* in my place. But I watched. I had so many cameras, I saw them brushing their teeth and kissing and eating crumby food and, ugh, fucking. I listened to almost their every word. Man, it's worse than I thought."

"Throw everything away. And throw the footage away, too!"

"I want revenge. If I could get away with it, I'd kill the guy." He paused for a moment, a new idea hitting him. "Or...I'd kill her, so he would suffer. Yeah, that's what I'd do."

Harry, lay on his back, on the couch, with his eyes closed, and imagined his thumbs clamped tightly on Lipschitz's throat as he stared, bug-eyed at Harry, knowing his smile would be the last thing Richard Lipshitz saw.

"That's intense. And scary," Liv said, trying to get through his haze of obsession. "It's starting to be too much for me. And for you. I love you and I need you to be happy again. C'mon Harry, snap out of it. Please?"

Harry had stopped listening and no longer heard anything she was saying. He continued, talking over her, "You should see this footage." He was ecstatic about what he'd captured, and though he wasn't consciously aware of it, the pain and anxiety of his discovery was getting him very high.

"It's like *you're* the one being tortured," Liv said.

Harry plowed on. "Maybe you should paint some of these images. Every frame is a masterpiece."

"Fuck no! I never want to see them. Let's go get something to eat."

"Eat? I don't want to eat. I'm not hungry. Really, I don't eat, anymore. This whole thing is eating me from the inside out. But I'll come over and watch you eat. I actually could use a break."

There was a long pause—not uncommon for phone conversations between Harry and Liz. This particular call had caught Liz in her studio. She continued painting silently, her earbuds in.

Harry remained on the couch, eyes closed, visualizing how he was going to use this golden material. "I'm going to write a screenplay about this," he dreamed out loud to Liv.

"That's just an excuse to keep spying." She was becoming exasperated with Harry's stubbornness and continued slapping paint on her canvas. "Maybe. I mean, I know. You're absolutely right. But know what? I feel more alive right now—right this minute, more than I've ever felt in my entire life.

Chapter 40

"You are to wait in the car until I call you. Got it?" barked Mistress Chunxx.

"Yes, Mistress," said her slave, Fido. He wasn't wearing his signature black leather gimp suit and his red, zippered hood had been replaced by a sporty chauffer's cap.

"And don't fuck up my car!" barked Chunxx, referring to the already rather buggered-up, late-model, maroon Chevy Impala sedan.

The obsequious doorman at 1011 Park Avenue, not unlike Fido, in his own way, scooted out to the street. He knowingly nodded and escorted Chunxx through the once-elegant entrance, to the elevator. She pushed 34 and imagined how elegant her life would become, having met a rich person like Georgia.

"Just think, I'll be living like this in no time," she muttered, closing her eyes and conjuring up images of a dream dungeon, teeming with submissives, slaves, theme rooms, and clones of herself—whipping and spitting and putting cigarettes out on all manner of tongues and faces and backsides of the wealthy gentlemen in need of discipline. All at her beck and call.

"I'll call it *The Sanguine Estate*," she dreamt out loud.

Two firm knocks and the door opened. Georgia stood, all smiles and nerves, holding a glass of Chardonnay in one hand and a cigarette pinched in the other. She wrapped an arm around Chunxx, careful not to spill her drink and the two air-kissed cheeks.

That's a heavy brew of perfume she's wearing, Georgia thought, as she pulled away, closing the door. "Please, come in to my humble lair," she said with a sweeping gesture. To the wide-eyed Chunxx, who grew up in a dozen foster homes, this was a palace. To have an apartment on Park Avenue! In reality, it was only a rent-controlled, shabbily furnished sublet, inherited from Georgia's dead Russian aunt, and the rent was only a few hundred dollars a month.

"Oh yes, it's such a sweet little pied-à-terre. I inherited it from my Uncle Dimitri, a Georgian prince exiled after those dreadful Bolsheviks did their business." Georgia told this tale to anyone who would listen. Both Chunxx and Lipschitz were taken in by this tidbit of misinformation. (Harry knew the real story, yet he enjoyed watching her con friends and strangers. He even allowed her to think she was conning him. Those stories about her family background, her education, and those dropped names. To him, her pathology was attractive, even sexually arousing.)

The women were on their third glass of Chardonnay. Georgia opened another magnum as they sat down to a very simple meal she fashioned from a head of romaine lettuce and a few slices of leftover chicken breast. Chunxx was in the process of revealing her plans for the ultimate dungeon.

"Can you imagine? All the rooms just like the old place on 37th Street—except new, with a few modern twists. You know, some white leather and chrome couches, maybe even dimmer switches!" she blathered. "And of course, a decent changing room for us."

"Like a green room," offered Georgia.

"Yeah, good idea. And we'll be on our own; no more subletting or working for the man. We could call it The Sanguine Estate. I thought of that on the way up in your elevator," gushed Chunxx.

"I love it!" Georgia lit another cigarette, now officially chain-smoking. "And I love this brainstorming! Working together will be such great fun."

Chunxx knew Gerogia was clueless, but at least she was rich and willing.

"I've worked out a plan, a very simple plan for purchasing our new facility," Georgia continued, finishing off her forth glass of wine. "It assumes leaving my investments in tact, other than the equity I have in my co-op, minus my living expenses for the rest of the year. I would end up with five hundred thousand minimum in the bank, invested for growth, income, and preservation of capital." Georgia's thoughts and words were beginning to slur as she reeled off a memorized regurgitation of Richard Lipschitz's ridiculous business plan.

"Mmmmmm..." responded Chunxx, confused. *Whatever, girl. As long as you've got the money, honey, it all sounds good to me*, she thought. "By the way, this chicken is delicious. What's for desert?" she asked, with a mouth full of food. "Please, continue."

Georgia ate almost nothing. She picked at a piece of romaine with little enthusiasm. Chunxx, on the other hand, dug in, eating everything that remained on Georgia's plate.

They opened another bottle of wine.

"Thanks for being so patient with me," Georgia said, "I so much want to get out of my skin, to molt, to change." Inebriated, she lit another cigarette from the end of the one she was smoking. "I have this debilitating problem with self-confidence. Especially to myself. And—guess what—no surprise...I have trouble following through on anything." Georgia took another swig of wine, emptying her glass for the eighth time, and with great force pulled the hot, bitter smoke through her cigarette. "You're probably thinking, this is just like Richard telling me he's wearing a rug, right?"

"He wears a toupee?" Chunxx chortled, her mouth full of romaine, chicken, and the tail end of the day-old baguette Georgia offered her at the last minute. "And this has what to do with The Sanguine Estate?"

"Well, I had no idea until he told me. What a surprise. I'd rather be wearing a rug than have *my* traits. The ones I just mentioned."

"Oh honey, a rug. That's too funny," Chunxx tittered.

"I'd rather have a bald head than my traits. I have to own who I am though, right? Whatever that means. Seems like meaningless words to me." She paused long enough to top off her wine glass, somehow getting back on topic. "Maybe we should just find a house to rent. Buying something just now does not seem like the right idea," Georgia slurred, shaking her head, "I can't do it."

Chunxx took a swig of her wine and lit up a Virginia Slim.

"Wait, honey. You need to follow through with this. And you know you'll get into it. You're attracted to it. Anyone can see that and you'll be good at it, too! It's a great lifestyle. You'll see. You'll make tons of money and I'll show you how. We can start out renting, if we have to. It's okay, I have a little money set aside that I can put in too, although, I thought you were loaded—"she probed, fidgeting nervously.

Georgia didn't respond, so Chunxx changed the subject, feigning levity. "Now pass me that bread! I just can't get enough!" She laughed smoke out her nose, pretending she hadn't noticed Georgia withdrawing at her question. *That's it. I'm gouging her for all she's worth,* schemed the now serious dominatrix to herself.

"I'm not ready to commit all of it, but I will put up some capital to start the project and get it going. I'm in," gulped Georgia, with fake confidence. "After all, I *am* a dog runner," she said, "I take care of five to ten dogs a week. Shit, if I can do that, why not?"

This news hit Chunxx in the face like a brick. *A fucking dog walker? Why had no one told me this?* She retained an outward calm while she sucked down a whole cigarette and polished off her glass of wine.

Chapter 41

"Look, it's perfect. It's owned by this Jewish school. I'm good with this. I'll do the negotiating. These are my people and I know how to talk to them. I'm the best rabbi finesser within five hundred miles of here." Lipschitz drank another gulp of his Starbucks macchiato grande, then chewed off a piece of his second cinnamon bun.

Richard was most happy when manipulating, conning and closing on a deal—any deal, really—from buying a bruised apple for less than retail all the way up to, in this case, renting a house. In his mind, he was a wild predator closing in on the kill; all deals and negotiations were primal. He pictured himself as a cheetah, ready to spring on an unsuspecting impala. He found what he thought was the perfect location for The Sanguine Estate: an old farmhouse in New Beauford, New York with at least a dozen rooms, along with an included barn.

Georgia, backtracking, reminded him, "Richard, I don't feel as though I am quite ready to purchase a property."

"No problem, we'll just rent for now." His mind moved a mile a minute. "Imagine; a torture chamber, a medieval room, a rubber room, an isolation chamber, a jail. We could do so much!" He calculated the fun of this project—mostly thinking of his own fun and pleasure. "So," he got down to business, "how much cash can you put up?"

Georgia looked away for a second, then back, looking Richard directly in the eye. "Twelve grand."

His jaw slackened as he gazed back at her, revealing those giant oversized capped teeth. He took a deep, disappointed breath and pretended not to miss a beat. "Okay then! I guess it's good enough for now. We can do it. *We can do this!*" The consummate optimist pumped himself up, trying to carry Georgia along with his feigned enthusiasm.

"Richard, I'm scared, but excited too. You'll have to help me. I need you by my side all the way on this. I don't know what I'm doing. What am I doing?" She held her head in her hands, almost crying. She was genuinely afraid.

What am I getting myself into, Georgia thought? These people think I'm wealthy, and twelve grand is more than half of my savings. Yet, maybe it's a good investment. And I could double my money—or more...or I could lose everything." Her shoulders slumped. She entered a spiral of negative thinking, going deeper and darker. This was a very familiar place. After all, it was her home more often than not.

Grabbing her by the shoulders and shaking her back to their business meeting, Richard reassured her. "You're doing the right thing, Mistress Coco. You're gonna see. This business venture is what you've been waiting for!"

His cockeyed optimism pulled her back, calming her enough that she nodded her head in agreement. "I still wonder about Harry though, and your family."

Richard couldn't completely hide his exasperation. "One thing at a time. Let's get this going. Don't worry so much. I'm calling Chunxx right now to get the ball rolling. Everything is good. Really. Fuck that creep you seem to care so much about. He can't hurt us as long as he doesn't know what we're up to. We changed our passwords, our identities. That piece of shit is harmless, and we do not want him in our lives any longer. Full stop! Got it?"

Having been duly slapped back into sobriety and pulled from her downward spiral, she responded quietly, "right." Her head automatically nodded several times.

"You're damn right I'm right! We're on, okay? Start the preparations! We're going to be rich, I'm telling you. This makes me hard! What a dream come true!" Richard was practically foaming at the mouth as he closed the deal. He laughed demonically.

Chapter 42

"This is what I'll need for the table: a piece of premium grade plywood. No, not pressure treated. Also, two six by sixes, eight feet long; four two by fours, eight feet long; fifty quarter inch by three and a half inch long lag bolts; a quart of dark brown stain and a quart of polyurethane. I'll pick up the casters. And if you could just think about what we'll need for the foothold on the cross…maybe a piece of two by twelve by about four feet long. It needs sanding, staining, sealing and mounting on the wall. Richard can finish it in about two hours. You can get everything we need at Home Depot." Chunxx, headset plugged into her iPhone, was in high gear, rattling off her latest list to Georgia, who was out running errands for The Sanguine Estate.

Making lists of things for other people to do was one of Chunxx's specialties. She checked her clipboard. The list was filled with everything from hardware to dildos. "Yes Georgia, and when you're done with that, swing over to Toys in Babeland and pick up an assortment of dildos, different sizes, and get yourself a strap-on harness. We need to upgrade you to something more professional. Most of our clients will require at least some degree of ass play, so maybe pick up a few butt plugs as well. And get back here ASAP, we need you to shoot some pictures for the website."

No sooner had the portly dominatrix clicked the end button on her conversation with Georgia, she was on to her next project. A graphic layout of the new brochure and website homepage had been neatly displayed, on the kitchen table, by one of her numerous slaves.

The Sanguine Estate: A household strictly run by
two elegant, dominant women.

This is a beautiful old farmhouse in the quiet Westchester County town
of New Beauford, New York.

A place like no other.

"There's a nice ring to that." This was Chunxx's dream come true, and her manic, perfectionist, obsessive-compulsive personality was in overdrive.

From the entrance and the foyer, one could only assume that whoever lived in this house was a normal, upstanding, solid citizen; a classic example of pure Shaker living. Enter the main bedroom on the first floor and it was a different story. A device in the center of the room, somewhat resembling a massage table, but suited for various torture games, was lit by one dimmed spotlight from above. The top was covered with black vinyl, and its legs and rails were made of sanded and stained four by fours, the color a walnut brown. Two other similarly constructed, clunky, homemade chairs with padded vinyl headrests and multiple tie-down straps connected to the legs and arms were off to one side of the table. On the other side of the room, two Home Depot early American reproduction wall sconces illuminated a St. Andrews cross made of bulky stained lumber, large enough to accommodate an adult male. Wide leather straps were attached to secure arms and legs.

The walls and ceiling of the room were dark maroon, as were the heavy drapes blocking the daylight. The space was absolutely stark, clean and neat as a pin and the air was permeated with odors of fresh plaster, latex paint and polyurethane, ammonia and Windex. The rest of the house was a flurry of orderly and organized activity.

With military precision, Chunxx snapped her fingers and directed more than a dozen volunteer slaves, sissy maids, and submissives as they fabricated, painted, and cleaned the various elements of the theme rooms. She breathed in the odors and sounds of construction, of progress, of discipline. "Mmmmm. Music to my nose and ears," she hummed.

On the floor of what was once a dining room, her favorite and long-time slave, Fido, opened boxes of mail-order dildos, ball gags, whips, paddles, clamps and all manner of sex toys. He fairly shook with anticipation and enthusiasm. He carefully organized them according to his mistress's strict instructions. As he pulled out a brand new hood, covered in zippers and snaps, with built in ball gag, he burst into tears of abject joy. He knew this one was his, as it was the exact one his beloved mistress had promised him.

Meanwhile, upstairs in the former master bedroom, Frank, Mistress Chunxx's submissive boyfriend, the carpenter of the group, fabricated a large man-sized wooden X, with precision, from two by sixes. Using a ratchet wrench, he twisted the lag bolts through the boards and screwed in place thick leather belts designed to secure wrists, ankles, upper arms, and waist. One of the volunteer submissives, was busily cleaning and dusting everything in the room while Frank worked. Chunxx's orders of strict cleanliness were to be maintained at all times.

Georgia arrived back from her errands and pulled into the driveway in the boss's beat up maroon Chevy Impala. She took in the sunny spring day, camera slung over her shoulder.

Chunxx stood in the rather substantial, unkempt back yard, surrounded by a tall, dense, ancient hedge of privet, admiring her newly acquired pony cart. Fido, using a Q-tip, cleaned the last few particles from its spokes. With two efficient gestures, she dismissed her slave with a finger snap.

"Now finish the rest of what you started in the kitchen," she ordered.

She summoned Georgia across the driveway for a serious chat. "I have wanted to have a structured and controlled household for a very long time. At first, the separation of emotions sounded cold and foreign to me, but I now realize that this is the most valuable part of the structure. Your relationship with Richard Lipschitz is a love relationship. It is impossible to combine a love relationship with a structured mistress/slave relationship. Informality—uncontrolled, default, casual intimacy—quickly erodes structure on both sides of the leash. It has a place, but I would keep in mind that although informality may be attractive at times, it can be very costly in the long run. Do I make myself clear?"

Chunxx stood at attention, eyes fixed on Georgia, who blinked, very obviously confused. "Yes, of course."

Georgia was in way over her head. With every command and order, diatribe and manifesto, her pull into the black hole that was Chunxx's world became stronger and more frightening. Yet, she felt sure there was no turning back. The two of them stood in silence. Frank approached, dressed like an Amish farm lady, wearing an ankle-length dark blue dress, black wig, and matching bonnet. He demurely slipped into the seat of the children's pony cart. Behind him trailed a large, pasty, new slave. Kola was a recent addition to Chunxx's group of submissives and slaves. He wore only a black jockstrap, hiking boots, and a horse harness. Prodded along by a good bit of scolding from Chunxx, he connected himself via the harness to the cart. Frank expertly grabbed the reigns and cracked them over Kola's soon to be red back, and off they trotted.

"Heyaaaa," coaxed Frank.

Fido joined the party by chasing after the cart, then, not being too terribly coordinated, jumping clumsily on. He wore adult diapers, a baby bonnet, white socks with sandals, and a strange little pink, crocheted blouse.

Georgia clicked photos of all of this. Perhaps something for posterity, or the website, she thought. She followed Chunxx through the house, shooting more as Chunxx posed in every room of the dungeon, sometimes with slaves or submissives beneath boots and whips, or wrapped in chains, or ball gagged and hobbled like farm animals.

Okay, this is fun, she thought to herself. Half an hour and hundreds of clicks later, she drained her third glass of Chardonnay as she put her camera equipment away.

Chapter 43

Georgia sat naked, sorting her recent photographs of The Sanguine Estate, while Richard, in black Speedo briefs and black knee socks, a patch of skin exposed through a hole in the heel, stood behind her. He pretended to look at the computer screen, while exclaiming how blown away he was by her photographs. Really, he mostly gazed down at her tight, perfect body. She was a far cry from his wife of sixteen years who'd birthed three kids and imbibed way too many pizzas, macs and cheese, and beers, he thought, as the late afternoon sun blasted through the west facing windows of 1011 Park Avenue.

"Nice shots of Chunxx," fawned Lipschitz, not really caring. He poured himself a third glass of Merlot, trying to catch up to Georgia in the drunk department. "Yeah, baby!" he shouted at the next photo—Chunxx wearing a heavy fur coat of some unknown species. She stood eyeball-to-eyeball with her boyfriend, Frank, who was naked, except for nipple clamps, a dog collar, and a leash grasped tightly in Chunxx's hand. Her eyes, like rivets, pierced his puppy-like, submissively loving gaze.

"You really nailed that moment," declared Richard, as though a cultured aesthete. He imagined himself an art critic. Or maybe he could even be a curator of photography at the Museum of Modern Art.

Georgia showed him several more photos of Chunxx posing in all of the newly renovated rooms. Chunxx in her vinyl nurse's outfit in the medical room, giving Frank an enema. Chunxx wearing her black

Marlon Brando motorcycle cap and oversized fake Gucci sunglasses, her bloated collagen lips painted bright red; her tight corset overflowing with breast blubber. Chunxx posing, arms crossed, thigh-high, black, vinyl stilettos stretched over her wide calves. Frank, in soft focus in the background, strapped and ball gagged on the walnut stained wooden cross he made himself.

"Wow!" declared Lipschitz, downing his forth glass of red wine, "You've got a real talent!" He stood behind Georgia, not even glancing at the computer screen. His attention was directed over her shoulder, at her firm silicone breasts. The fact they were fake actually excited him more than if they had been real. He reached around to her right and cupped her breast in his palm. Her nipple hardened as he twirled it between his stumpy thumb and forefinger. He reached around the other side, performing the same procedure on the other breast.

"Stop it!" She slapped his hands away. "We have to keep this separate," she protested, remembering Chunxx's lecture. Yet, she couldn't help but feel the excitement building in the pit of her stomach and in that magic area slightly above her mons pubis. She pushed him away. "I want you to see some of *my* pictures, of me. Harry helped me shoot them. Well, he did the shooting and I directed him."

The mention of Harry's name immediately killed the mood, and pushed Lipschitz to the brink of a jealous rage. He gulped down the dregs in his glass and walked into the kitchen. There, he sucked several large mouthfuls directly out of the bottle and poured the remainder into his glass.

Pull yourself together, Lipschitz reminded himself. "No temper, be professional," he said quietly, through gritted teeth. "Harry's fucking with me here, and you *cannot* fuck with a mindfucker!" This thought reassured him. He reflected back a few months ago, to his lecture at T.E.S.

The Schadenfruede Society, known as TSS, was created in the late 1960's by and for those in the world of bondage, discipline, and sadomasochism. Lipschitz was an active member and a regular lecturer. Considering himself an old pro, he'd been at this game for over twenty years. He often bragged to Georgia that there was not one sexual, or BDSM experience, he hadn't tried at least once, and most were an ongoing part of his usual repertoire.

In front of what looked like an abandoned storefront, a sign on an easel outside the door read:

Mindfucking

Lecture and slideshow
By Sir Richard Lipschitz

There were about twenty TSS members, of all shapes and sizes, sitting in the makeshift classroom. The students ranged from Goth to suburban, with one paraplegic, a few hefty lesbians wearing blue jeans and tank tops, a wrinkled man sporting an eye patch, as well as three bald, forty-something men wearing identical flannel work shirts, faded blue jeans, rings of keys clipped to their beltloops, and tan work boots. The classroom was cordoned off by homemade, unfinished sheetrock partitions. The space was part of an industrial loft rented out to multiple groups at the same time, so other events were happening in separate areas. Sounds from an Off-Off-Broadway musical rehearsal filtered in.

Lipschitz fussed with his computer and the projector, trying to get his Power Point presentation working. Finally, the evening's host, Stosh, a middle-aged man dressed in black jeans, his stomach cascading over his belt and all but hiding his large brass "Stosh" buckle, strolled in front of the audience. He had bird legs and a beer gut, dyed, black, stringy hair, and his arms were covered with tats. The guy, dressed as a ballerina, controlling the light switch gave the nod that the show was ready to begin.

"Hello everybody!" enthused Stosh. "Thanks for coming tonight. As you know, our lecture is about the fine art of mindfucking. And there's no one more qualified to present this topic than the master himself. Our own illustrious, capricious, notorious, horrendously outrageous Sir Richard—Dick—Lipschitz. Let's put our hands together and welcome this weathered veteran of sadomasochism."

Everyone clapped enthusiastically, and there were a couple of whistles. Georgia, looking very WASPy—a square jawed, proper real estate lady, entered from the back and perched at the rear of the classroom. Lipschitz, the only person in the room wearing a suit, tie and nametag, was completely in his element. Even his corporate look was kinky, in his mind. Exuding false modesty, he trotted up to the lectern, tapped the mic to test it, and, while giving Georgia a bold wink, began his presentation.

"Is everybody ready to get mindfucked? Just kidding. But seriously, tonight we're talking about being the top in this equation. We're talking about being in control of someone who has no idea that they are part of our game. Can we dim the lights please?"

The first slide came up—an orange background with black letters.

What is a mindfucker?

The next slide showed a picture of Lipschitz, grinning.

The audience responded with laughs, applause, and a whistle. Someone yelled out, "You go, girl!"

The next slide read: A mindfucker is a student of human weakness and vulnerability, using these traits to create false beliefs and emotional chaos.

Next slide: What is Mindfucking?

"You ask, what is mindfucking?" Lipschitz is in full professor mode, reading verbatim from the slide. "Mindfucking is an inherently dominant and aggressive act of psychological violence, used with the intension to harm and inflict pain. Mindfucking ranges from being simply mischievous to homicidal."

Next slide: How Do We Mindfuck?

"How do we mindfuck?" he asked rhetorically. "We must first prey on the weaknesses of the victim. The best victims are actually complicit in their own demise. For example: someone who is prone to jealousy is easily made jealous by suggestions of infidelity. Lying is another direction to get into, as long as the victim wants to believe what is being said. In a certain sense, all mindfucking is, at least in part, self-inflicted."

Next slide. Our goal: to drive the victim crazy.

"Our goal is to drive our victims nuts! Got it?" asked the professor, strutting back and forth in front of the group.

The students responded with applause, and another "Yeah baby!"

The memory receded and Lipschitz talked himself down, sotto voce. "You almost got me there, Harry. The whole jealously thing. Well, who's her boyfriend now? Who's with her, building a dream dungeon, bitch?" Returning to Georgia, at the computer, he gently placed his hands on her shoulders and kissed the top of her head, ever so softly.

"You're just so beautiful and hot," he cooed. "You will be the prize dominatrix."

"Really?" she asked, fishing.

"Yes, and I will teach you how."

"You already are. I'm counting on it, Richard."

"I will teach you the correct way, the safe way. In fact," he said. He fished in his inside jacket pocket that had been carefully hung over the back of a chair, "Here's a list of dos and don'ts I compiled for you earlier today." He showed her the neatly typed list, then began reading it himself:

1. Always interview future clients first
2. Bring a notepad
3. Keep the meeting to fifteen minutes
4. Do not do a session right after the meeting
5. If they have their own toys, they can bring them
6. They need to leave a deposit of fifty dollars
7. They must start off slow, and only over time explore different aspects of the life-style
8. Do not tell them too much about yourself. Do not get personal —*important!*
9. If they are out of shape, offer them diet training
10. Call your payment a "consultation fee."

Georgia blinked and nodded silently, as she reread the list. This was going to be her new career and she was optimistic—and horrified—at the prospect that she would fail, and experience yet another humiliating defeat.

Chapter 44

On a quiet, sunny day, in the sleepy hamlet of New Beauford, a short train ride just north of Manhattan, trees swayed gently in a warm breeze, a monarch butterfly floated clumsily, searching for nectar; two male, red-breasted robins fluttered toward one another, vying for domination; all the usual things were happening. Moms transported kids, yellow labs, golden retrievers, groceries and soccer balls in Volvo station wagons and myriad European sport utility vehicles. Unsuspecting, they passed by the sweet old farmhouse, that was now The Sanguine Estate, on its first day open for business. Inside, under a single dim spotlight, in the pristine dungeon, curtains drawn, Georgia and Chunxx sat quietly, drinking coffee and smoking Virginia Slim menthol cigarettes. Georgia was dressed, for the first time, as a real, professional dominatrix: thigh-high, black, vinyl stilettos, fishnet stockings, black leather hot pants, and a borrowed red leather corset that was slightly too big. *I am so fucking anxious and these god damned menthol cigarettes*, she thought. *Maybe I've had too much coffee.*

Chunxx, the old pro, was even more anxious and excited about the renovation. She analyzed a few last-minute details, then suggested that Georgia pick up some more things from Toys in Babeland the next time she was in the city.

"And more lube," she offered. "Get a price on that new sex chair. It might be fun, and Frank could build a cage around it. And that radio bit we did last week? Why don't you edit that nicely so we can put it on the website?"

Georgia accompanied Mistress Chunxx to a makeshift studio in Brooklyn for an appearance on The Radio Dom Show. While this was to be a live call-in segment, they would be videotaping everything to use on the Mistress Chunxx website, as promotion for The Sanguine Estate. The show was pretty low-budget and not many people listened, but the video would be great advertising, according to Chunxx.

The two sat next to each other as the camera sloppily zoomed in. Moon-faced, tubby, inflatable sex doll, Chunxx rolled her eyes, exasperated at the lameness of the questions, as Georgia, face tighter than a snare drum, having reaped the full benefits of her face lift, bubbled with fake enthusiasm and pretended to be at ease in her new world, even though she didn't understand much about it.

Maybe I'm supposed to act like an old whore who's seen it all, she thought to herself, comfortable in any situation. Try as she might to work herself up, the camera revealed a pathetic creature—out of place, squirming, and insecure.

> **Chunxx:** Hello there.
> **Caller:** Hi, I'm Frank.
> **Georgia:** How are you?
> **Caller:** I'm fine, how...
> **Chunxx:** What's your fantasy, Frank? What would you never do in your wildest dreams?
> **Caller:** Well, I guess I'd like to...
> **Chunxx:** C'mon big boy, spit it out. Or would you rather I spit it out on your naked ass?
> **Georgia:** (quiet tittering)
> **DJ:** So, what do you think of these dominatrix ladies?
> **Caller:** Well, I think I'd like to meet them.
> **Georgia:** Hi Frankie boy.
> **DJ:** Do you have a question for these ladies?

Caller: Um, yeah. What size are your boobies?
Chunxx: Ah, 40 double D
Caller: And they're natural, right?
Chunxx: (silence): Ah, ya...sure.
Georgia: (volunteered): I'm 32 C...

The Radio Dom Show continued on for another ten minutes as the two dominatrices pretended to enjoy themselves, fielding calls from their lame clientele.

"So, okay," barked Chunxx,. "We have ten minutes before our first client arrives. I've worked with him for years. His kink is being an adult baby."

"A baby?" Georgia asked. I can whip the shit out of Richard, but a baby, she wondered?

"Yep, that's what I said. You bought that case of Depends, right?"

"No, Fido did that errand. He insisted," responded Georgia, bracing to be reprimanded after not personally attending to a request by the Maitresse, herself.

"No matter," continued Chunxx. "He gets off wearing diapers, he likes being naked. He likes wearing a leash like a little kid would wear at the mall. Try that new collar. Oh wait, here he comes. No names, okay?"

A slight, elderly gentleman tapped on the front door. He was Patrician, with a shock of feathery grey hair, neatly combed and parted. He was dressed like a WASPy, pro-bono lawyer in a well-worn, hounds tooth, tweed jacket, faded red bowtie, with a navy blue silk pocket square, neatly in place.

"I hope this is the right place," he whined to himself. No one answered. The game had already begun. Finally, he tested the knob, found it unlocked, and poked his head into the foyer, "Hello..." he called out gently.

He received no answer as he walked through the foyer and minced his way into the kitchen, where Georgia and Chunxx ignored him.

"Please help me," he pleaded pitifully, playing the game. "Am I in the right place, Mommy?"

"Mommy! You moron!" Chunxx dug in, "You're in the right place alright, you fucking brat. Now crawl over to my new assistant Coco, and show her what I've been teaching you for the past ten years. Kiss her feet!"

Immediately obeying, he got down on all fours and crawled over to Georgia, who recoiled a bit.

"Mistress, I've been so bad. Mommy sent me here. I need to learn more."

"She's waiting and I'm watching, you slimy fuckwad. C'mon now, stay on all fours, you bottom feeder!" Chunxx commanded, teaching Georgia by example.

She nodded to Georgia. "Okay Mistress Coco, he's all yours. Don't spare him. He needs more than a spanking."

Georgia weakly pointed to a room off the kitchen. The baby room featured an oversized crib, a few large stuffed animals, an unopened box of Depends, and some pacifiers, clinically placed in a white enameled medical tray on the floor.

"Okay," she rallied in a forced stern voice, "you come with me. Now!" She planted a tentative kick on his ass as they entered the room.

Georgia was shaky and unsure. She cracked her riding crop lightly on the palm of her hand and told him to get undressed. "Now look, you little cocksucker—don't you touch me!" She put on two pairs of rubber gloves, one over the other, then grabbed his neck and buckled a spiked dog collar around it, far too gently.

Meanwhile, a very drunk Richard Lipschitz arrived at the back entrance to the house. He parked his car half on and half off the driveway, leaving tire skid marks as he slammed on the brakes. He half-fell out of the car and stumbled up to the door. "Where the fuck-is-she? Needtoshee-her," he slured. "Getouddamy way," he scolded the locked door in a drunken garble.

Chunxx stormed over to find out what was going on. Whipping open the door, she screamed, "What the fuck are you trying to do, asshole? Shut the fuck up! She's with a client! Now settle down. Dimwit!" Chunxx slammed him in the face with her elbow, Krav Maga style. He reeled backward, passing out in a heap on the back porch.

Chapter 45

Two days after his drunken scene on the opening day of The Sanguine Estate, Richard Lipschitz showed up, unannounced, at 1011 Park Avenue. Georgia had been in isolation, not answering his emails or phone calls since the episode. She drank steadily, alternating vodka and Chardonnay and chain smoked Marlboros, having sworn off menthols forever.

Isolation was boring, of course, so when she heard the lock on the door clicking open, she put out her cigarette and lifted her robe, enough to expose her naked ass, and pretended to be asleep on the couch. Lipschitz let himself in and peered around the corner. He was dressed in his business-casual uniform: white Izod-golf pro shirt and tan chinos with no socks. He obediently removed his dark brown penny loafers and tiptoed over to Georgia, lifted up her feet, sat down, put them on his lap and began massaging a foot with his stumpy, well trained, fingers. He worked the sides of her heel and Achilles tendon, an electric connection he knew to fire directly into her clitoral nerve endings. Meanwhile, he stared dumbstruck at her smooth, slender, perfect, twelve-year-old Swedish boy's ass. Its naked presence sent high voltage pulses down the shaft of his growing rod, which tunneled upward and pulled slightly to the left.

A minute of that, and he carefully lifted the massaged foot up and into his gaping maw, past the oversized, super-white, capped dentures, where he deep-throated it like so many cocks from his past.

"I thought you said you would teach me the right way and the safe way?" Georgia's voice was barely audible, but angry. Without looking up, she whimpered, "What did you think you were doing? Yelling, making a scene... That was my first session. Ever. The opening day of The Sanguine Estate. What the fuck, Richard?" Her eyes squeezed tighter as she retreated into a fetal position. "Leave me alone."

They both knew she didn't really want to be alone. She needed to be held, needed to be naked, needed to feel his cock inside her. She was too drunk to stay angry and too stubborn to crack open.

"I am so sorry," he lied, searching for a chink in her armor, calculating just how to manipulate the situation. "I thought I could do this with you. And I will, but not like this." He paused, pulling her out of her crouched position, and began the foot massage again. He knew her weakness: the soft inner arch that, when manipulated correctly, was a direct conduit to her medial-forebrain-bundle....blasting dopamine into her central nervous system. That combined with all the consumed alcohol and, he assured himself, she would be his again.

"We need to go it alone. It's got to be just you and me. I can't take not being there with you. I have to be with you." He paused, continuing the foot massage, kissing the top of each foot. "Let's get out of this. I have to be there with you, watching. Like you are doing it for me and me alone."

Georgia sat up, yanking her feet back. "What are you even saying?" She took a swig of vodka, then lit a cigarette. "You got me into this! How are we supposed to get out of it? And what about Mistress Chunxx?!" Lipschitz avoided eye contact, sliding into his poor me posture. "Just tell her you want out. Tell her you can't do it."

"I can't," she sniveled. "I mean, I really can't. I really don't think I can do it. It's not a lie. I still don't feel comfortable with her. It's true. And I would rather do this with you, but she'd never go for it. Do you have any idea how pissed she'd be? I'm afraid of her, and so is everybody else. She spent her life savings on this. And she's into me for twelve grand now," Georgia sobbed. That twelve grand was *her* life savings as well.

Did Richard still think she was wealthy? Now what was she supposed to do? Was she supposed to be a dog runner for the rest of her life? Georgia thought back to that first Craig's List ad she'd followed up. Gunther, and those two, crazy Rottweilers. Sure, I love to run, she'd thought. That was until her arms were practically ripped out of their sockets.

Georgia quit real estate after spending a year not selling one apartment; being abused, belittled and berated by bosses, clients and even her parents, "You are way too old and passive to have one ounce of success in this business," scolded her father; a failed real estate broker himself; her mother nodding in complete agreement; a defeated Georgia called it quits.   Angrily acknowledging that her father was right, Georgia left the business, having failed yet again to commit, to stick with it, to follow through...to succeed. She became a *floater*, a person other real estate brokers refer to, someone who can't seem to find leads; an unproductive parasite; a pariah; an outsider; someone to stay away from; bad energy; bad vibes. And now, struggling once again, feeling broke and useless and depressed, with her last bit of energy, she managed to find a "position" as a dog runner. "Well, I love dogs and I run almost every day...why not..." she mused, as she answered the add on Craig's List.

At 6:00 AM, the dog owner, a tall blonde Aryan male, dark blue linen suit, starched white shirt, was on his cell phone, waiting impatiently for his employee to arrive. "You're late...and you know that you are not indispensable!" He yelled into the phone. The two massive black and tan Rottweilers lunged savagely toward an elderly black man passing cautiously in front of the brownstone.

"Omar! Friedrich! Halt! Platz!" he commanded. They quietly obeyed and sat, panting in anticipation of their morning run.

Five minutes later, Georgia showed up, locked her bike, and apologized profusely. She was still quite hung over from a dinner with Chunxx and had very little sleep as well.

"How can you do this to me?" barked Mr. Deutschland as he handed the beasts on leashes over to Georgia. She, in her skin tight black jogging shorts and skimpy top, backed away like a subservient slave. The giant, aggressive, alpha male Rottweilers charged toward the East River, setting the pace of what was to be a five mile run. Georgia was pulled, with great force, by the two very savage-looking dogs, while several early morning pedestrians dove out of their way.

They galloped on tree lined sidewalks, crossed mostly empty streets, the city just beginning to wake up. A few after-hours drunks staggered out of the way, looking blankly at nothing. It was hard to notice much with the breakneck pace the dogs had set. Having Finally arrived at the East River, they headed south, staying on the paved walkway, very close to the FDR Drive. She was surrounded by cement, steel, tractor trailers, and the constant noise of the elevated highway above. Here she was, a petite, middle aged, blonde with two massive black and tan, unfixed male Rottweilers...was she fucking nuts? Maybe dog *walking* would have been a better choice.

Chapter 46

The next day, the Lexus barreled west on I-95, heading nowhere in particular. Richard Lipschitz was still unemployed, yet he dressed up every morning in his rumpled, Burlington Coat Factory business suit, and pretended to go to work. Aggressively weaving through rush hour traffic, he fussed with the volume knob on his car stereo, listening to one of his favorites, Lance Romance. His phone rang and he glanced at the caller ID. Georgia. He paused the CD.

"So...did you do as I instructed?"

Big sigh. "I told her I wanted out and wanted my money back. She went ballistic, then said that there is absolutely no way that she will ever pay me back. Ever."

Lipschitz processed this information for a few seconds. "Well, guess what? I'm going to turn her in."

"You're what?" asked Georgia.

"I'm going to turn her in. Period. Full stop."

"To the police? What about us? How could you do that? That's a line I don't think I could ever cross."

"We don't have any other choice, Richard said. "The way I see it, it's the only way out." Lipschitz, shifted into full conspiracy mode.

"You could do that?" Georgia asked, in disbelief.

"Watch me. Now the fun begins. I'll call you later." He stepped on the gas, cranked up the volume, and high fived an imaginary passenger.

He raced down the highway, letting out a visceral war whoop as Lance kicked back in with his commentary on three-ways.

"If you've ever dreamed of a three-way...and I'm sure you have, here's a little advice. There are a couple elements to this seduction: attraction and comfort. Let's assume that you, my student and stud, want to involve two girls. Girl number one should already be at least a fuck buddy (someone who knows you and is familiar and comfortable with you). Girl number two should be her friend; someone she trusts. You, the seduction pro, have to get into their heads a bit and be somewhat aggravating, and be an ever so slightly obnoxious asshole. Get on their nerves so that they feel bonded together against you. (Of course this has all been planned in advance with your fuck buddy.) The game has to be fun and silly and not scary in any way. Just go with the flow and be sure to lubricate with a few shots of vodka. Soon you'll have to kiss and make up, then offer girl number one a foot massage. She accepts then gives girl number two something similar perhaps working up a leg or two, hinting at eroticism. All the while you are talking about the joys of experimentation and living for the moment, and how beautiful you two girls look together and now it's time for a group hug. Soon you begin making out with girl number one then sweetly, delicately bring in number two. Good luck!

Chapter 47

Five days later, Harry's friend Liv was going through her yoga routine on a large foam mat. She was in the cavernous gym at Chelsea Piers, a giant early 20th century steel-beam, former industrial pier, now a state-of-the-art fitness center. The space was practically empty as Harry sidled up and slid in front of her, with a folder of printed emails and a newspaper, opened to the front page of *The New York Post*. On it was a terrible close up of Chunxx being led away in handcuffs in grainy black and white.

Mansion Mistress Busted:
Cops Collar Whip Queen of Westchester.

"What? No! What did you do, Harry?" Liv asked in total disbelief. She sat up from her pose and grabbed the newspaper away from him. "You did this? You called the cops?"

Harry shook his head and grinned broadly in silence.

"What? Really? Is this them?"

"Yes. No joke. Lippy turned them in. He's such a fucking rat. He started this whole thing and then just turned on it and called the police."

"It's insane."

"I told you the guy is evil."

"How do you know it was him? What happened to them? Harry....are you still in?"

Harry looked down, quiet.

"Harry, are you still checking e-mail? You are. You gotta stop," Liv pleaded. "You're addicted. This is fucked up. You're going to go crazy. You gotta get a hold of yourself. Come back. It's too dark. Find the sweetness again."

Harry retorted, "Yes. I'm in. Just occasionally though," he lied. "And get this, they even sent her a hundred dollars to help with her legal fee fund. After they ratted her out!"

"Oh, Harry." Liv was shocked.

"They actually emailed each other about this. Lipschitz said, '*It's in the mail. Now you can relax and enjoy yourself.*' Then she said '*Did you check the spelling of the police chief's name?*' Here. Check out these emails." Harry opened his folder to a page containing two printed emails.

From: Georgia Pendleton gnabokov@gmail.com
To: Richard Lipschitz lipschitz@optonline.net
Subject: did you check the spelling of his name?

Now off to the gym!! Keep my panties on and that tampon inserted!!

From: Richard Lipschitz lipschitz@optonline.net
To: Georgia Pendleton gnabokov@gmail.com
Subject: It's in the mail

I almost drove right past the Estate on the way to mail our anonymous letter. Thought I should drop it in a box in Beauford Hills. Relax and enjoy yourself tonight and don't even think about what we are doing to Chunxx. She deserves this. If you need to talk or a hug, I'll be in the car. Just call.
XOXO

"And get a load of this letter." Under his breath, he read the letter to Liz:
Dear Chief Mendel,

I am a long time resident of Beauford Hills.

I have raised my family here and enjoy the community spirit of our town. I also appreciate greatly the security your fine police department provides. Recently it has come to my attention that a home, very close to mine, is doing business as some sort of brothel. And is being advertised on the web under the domain name of www.thesanguineestate.com. For months, I've noticed a flow of different cars in and out of the property that seemed suspicious. I have noticed the second floor remains dark, with a reddish glow. I did a bit of research, but couldn't prove anything. I am appalled that a home owned by the yeshiva might have business being conducted on the premises that could be of a sexual nature. I can't imagine that the yeshiva is actually aware, if indeed this activity is occurring. Before this they rented the house to a group of workers who were messy and noisy, but now this. Chief Mendel, you and I know each other, but I also know this letter could be used as something more than just a tip. I prefer that it remain a tip and I prefer to remain anonymous. But as a citizen of Beauford Hills, I ask you to investigate. This is an issue of safety, morals and values. My guess is that the house is not zoned for business anyway. But if there is business going on and it is of the nature I suspect it is, I would very much like to see action taken. I choose to bring up my family here because of the wholesome environment. Again I express my gratitude for your service to the community. Thank you.

Harry slowly shook his head. "I watched this happen in slow motion. I saw them set her up a month ago and now the headlines. You just can't make this stuff up."

Harry recalled the evening TV news coverage: The Sanguine Estate, filled with cops as Chunxx sat defiantly in a chair, questioned by two plainclothes officers. The door was kicked in, on camera, even though it wasn't locked. The rooms were methodically trashed. The news camera closely followed the action, crudely lighting its own path.

In his imagination, behind the scenes, cops smacked each other with dildos, laughed and howled, holding them over their dicks. They tried on the leather masks, whipped each other, tied each other up, and just basically enjoyed sadomasochism. They probably had a good time ripping down curtains and destroying all of Chunxx's painstaking work. The camera caught Chunxx looking at the destruction and sobbing, as she was handcuffed and led through the humiliating gauntlet of media and spectators.

Snapping Harry out of his daydream, Liv reprimanded him. "You have got to stop this. Stop spying. What you're doing is illegal. Do you want to go to jail? Those two will do anything to anybody. Look at what they did to one of their own. Imagine what they would do to you. If you insist on going online, at least find a new girlfriend on the internet. Everybody's doing it."

Harry held the *New York Post*, studying the headlines and the humiliating pictures of Chunxx's perp walk. "Okay. You're right. Good idea...I should probably move on and get a real life," he half-heartedly agreed.

"I didn't mean it that way Harry. You're a wonderful, talented, creative, smart and cool guy. Don't waste your time on these lowlifes," she said, "Find another love."

Chapter 48

Natasha answered the door. Having claimed to be forty-four on her Match.com profile and posted pictures of a younger, happier time, she was, in fact, probably much closer to sixty. She wore a dark blue, wool pinstripe suit over a white silk blouse with a very Eastern European, and oddly baroque, collar. It looked like a crocheted doily swiped from the back of some granny's easy chair, he thought. The blouse was mostly unbuttoned and revealed way too much cleavage and gobs of costume jewelry. Her eye makeup would have put all the whores in Vegas to shame. She looked Harry up and down, dressed in his usual uniform of blue jeans and a black T-shirt.

"Oh," she stammered as they exchange terrified glances, "I must get my coat." She closed the door with Harry still outside, and he seriously considered running away, just as Liv's number appeared on his ringing phone.

"Hey beloved, my fave GF! I'm on a date, actually, in Brooklyn." Harry considered what he's got himself into with equal parts pride and shame.

Liv laughed, "No flies on you, Casanova."

"C'mon, don't laugh, this was your idea. Can I call you back later?"

"Of course. Who's the lucky girl?"

"Someone named Natasha. A total train wreck of a nightmare of a train wreck. But at least food for the screenplay. Now shut up, dear. Here she comes." He switched off the phone and pressed record on his hidden digital audio recorder.

Natasha returned, wearing a leather and lynx fur coat even though it was a mild seventy degrees out. Her hair was clumped in bottle-blonde strings, but the dark roots indicated a dire need for a bit more color work. Or possibly a new colorist altogether, if there *was* one to begin with. Her face was puffy and creased, and Harry had the urge to ask her what sort of substances she had been abusing lately—but gallantly refrained. They walked at her snail's pace toward the restaurant she had chosen.

At a complete loss for words, Harry prodded her forward, one inch at a time.

"This used to be a Laundromat, right?" he lamely attempted. There was no reply. This whole date would be a wash if there was nothing on the recorder. He had to coax the depressed, or medicated, or just plain nuts Natasha to say something—a grunt, anything.

Finally she did. "I dunno. Do you like my coat?"

"Ah, yeah? I had no idea this street had become so hip. Cafes, little shops. It's quite nice actually. And what exactly is the architectural history of this area?"

"What?"

Harry loathed her slow pace and disinterest in ideas. Not that his ideas were anything spectacular, but at least words would fill the uncomfortable void. They reached the restaurant and she waited to have the door held open for her. Playing along, reluctantly, he grumbled to himself, "Shit, this could be a really long night."

Natasha removed her coat, forcing him to help her before they sat down. Her pale bosom flowed, undulating in slow motion, from the mostly unbuttoned blouse. As she hit the seat, the Jell-O inside her giant breasts jiggled lazily, then settled in for a long meal, heaving slightly as she chewed on one of the bread sticks. The banquette framed her in red crushed velvet and fake gold leaf—the décor of a Wild West brothel.

"You look absolutely, um, baroque." grasped Harry.

"What's that?" she asked. "I am from an ancient Georgian lineage; Russian royalty.

"Royalty?"

"Yes, and I speak five languages fluently."

"Fluently? That's impressive. Say something in Russian. Do you speak Russian?"

"Yes, but not now. You wouldn't understand anyway. But once I made a fortune."

"Really, doing what?"

"Two hundred and fifty thousand dollars."

"Doing what?"

"Doesn't matter. Here comes the waiter."

An attitudinal hipster leaned into the table, "And what can I get for you?"

"I'll have the cheesecake and Pellegrino."

"And for you, sir?" he asked with a touch of irony.

"Pellegrino. Thank you."

Harry was amazed at the cartoon character sitting in front of him and he couldn't wait to get away, but realized he would have to settle in until the cheesecake was eaten.

"I just got off a sixty day fast. I have been taking care of my mother, who is bipolar, and all I had to eat for six months was apple strudel. I gained so much weight I had to fast."

"Yeah, but now you're getting cheesecake."

"Yeah, just this once," she deadpanned. Without a moment's pause, she said, "I had a nasty boyfriend not too long ago. He wouldn't even pick me up from the airport after I had been with my mother all that time."

The Pellegrino and cheesecake arrived and she kept talking. "African American. He was a real pain. Not at all a gentleman, like I deserve."

Harry looked up at the waiter, who was clearly amused by the two incongruous characters at his table, and thanked him.

She continued without skipping a beat, "After all I am very passionate and I'm capable of great success. This guy, my old boyfriend, was abusive. He was in the military and taught martial arts and actually threatened to kill me."

"He threatened to kill you?"

"Yes, but as I said, I am very passionate and so the whole thing was very hot in every way."

As Natasha babbled on about herself, Harry drifted off—not in some spaced-out daydream—he actually fell asleep, slipping into a narcoleptic, euphoric escape. As his unconscious head tipped forward, a sudden sharp poke on his right hand snapped him awake.

"You fell asleep!" she scolded in a raspy, boiling voice, slowly pulling the fork away from his hand.

"Ya-no...was just listening with my eyes closed," he lied.

The check was discretely slipped to Harry, who left forty bucks in cash. Natasha stood, waiting for her fur coat to be slipped over her shoulders. As Harry complied, he wondered how anyone with her level of body fat could bear dressing so warmly on such a humid evening.

As they left the restaurant, by some miracle, there he was. The "boyfriend" stood across the street, arms folded, staring straight at them both.

Harry swallowed, nervous.

Natasha yelled out, "Hey asshole, I want you to meet someone."

The boyfriend scowled, assessing his escape route, and then shifted into high gear, speed walking out of there.

"Asshole," screamed Natasha, "I'm talking to you. Get back here. What are you afraid of?"

"Maybe you shouldn't antagonize the guy," suggested Harry.

The boyfriend jogged away into the night as Harry breathed a sigh of relief, though he wondered why a black-belt martial artist would be afraid of him—or this woman. They walked in silence, back to her apartment. On the sidewalk, in front of her place, he refused the offer to come in for a martini, a look at her etchings, and a play date with her five cats.

"Five? Oh, I can't. Sorry. I am really allergic to cats."

"I don't believe it. Just one martini? It won't hurt you. You don't have to stay long. C'mon," she practically begged.

"Ah, no thank you. Really, I have to go. It's been a long day and I am really allergic to cats. So, good-night. I had a great time."

Reluctantly accepting defeat, Natasha sighed, "All right. But next time you're coming up. And I don't believe you're allergic."

He cleared his throat and turned to leave. "I am," he whispered. It took all the restraint he could muster not to sprint toward the nearest subway stop.

Finally, he found himself on the Q train, heading back to the safety of Manhattan. As the train rose above ground, on the bridge, the vast wall of warm city lights invited him home.

Chapter 49

A few days later, Harry was again in dating mode and, on his way to the subway. He was on the phone with Liv, listening to her tell him about a painting she was having some trouble with.

"I think the background's too light. I've used a green that I really can't stand, but I think it needs to be there. Oh, Harry, I don't know. Should I change it to blue? What do you think?"

Harry wasn't paying enough attention and lost the train of the conversation. Actually, he had mostly been ignoring her, obsessed with himself, as usual. He interrupted her, "Yeah, I'm going to meet Prudence. We met for coffee last week and ended up having dinner."

Liv realized he hadn't heard anything she'd said. Yep, situation normal. She gave in to her dear neurotic friend, and listened.

"Yeah, I like her. She's nice. Nothing too serious. She has kids that she seems to care way too much about. Grown ones. Anyway, I'll talk to you later. What are you doing tonight?"

"Harry, I was just trying to explain the predicament I'm in with this painting! What do you think I'm doing tonight?"

"Okay. Okay," he laughed. "I'll talk to you later."

"You seem to be taking this online dating thing pretty seriously."

"Yeah, I think this is my tenth date this week."

"That's a lot of dates, Harry. It's a little... It's kind of..."

"Hey, I'm obsessive. What can I say?"

This was their second date and Prudence decided it might be fun to get together and read their works in progress. She'd been working on a short story and Harry told her about a project he'd been working on, although he hadn't told her much. She could tell he was as obsessed with his piece as she was with hers. She suggested they meet at her apartment and take turns reading their work aloud to one another.

Harry arrived on time for this first visit to her apartment. Prudence gave him a peck on the cheek and sat him down on the couch. She brought out a pot of herbal tea and finger sandwiches and carefully placed them on the coffee table in front of Harry. He glanced around the tiny studio apartment. The place was crammed with fabric scraps and yarn, knick-knacks and clutter—a hodgepodge of unfinished artsy-craftsy projects. The cramped quarters triggered the memory of a bed and break-fast somewhere in Maine or Vermont where he attempted to stay once. The lavender potpourri, flannel lampshades, and off-the-charts mold spore count caused such trauma that Harry ended up spending the night in his car, curled up in the back seat, swatting mosquitoes.

Harry had a cup of overly floral tea and a bite of a soggy, mostly cream cheese sandwich while they chatted a bit about their last date. Prudence talked about her habit of getting up before dawn to make a pot of her favorite tea and write for a few hours before getting ready for work at some office. Harry wasn't really paying much attention.

"I'll just start, shall I? Prudence said."

Harry nodded. "Sounds good."

"It was a cold and windy New Hampshire night last fall when the state police knocked on the door looking for my teenaged son. Shocked and dismayed, I mistakenly let them in and called to Morgan. He was in his room with the lights out, headphones clamped to his ears, listening to his favorite rock and roll group, Metalflake."

Call me a nomad,
a wanderer, a vagabond,
anything you choose,
leave me alone,
all alone to lose.

Harry vaguely remembered a distant Metalflake lyric and began to hear the familiar strains to *Vagabond Loser*. As the song played in his head, Prudence continued her reading, completely unaware that her utterly sincere voice thinned to a muffled whisper as Harry drifted off into his own vivid fantasy.

In a dimly lit dungeon, something like Doctor Frankenstein's laboratory, Richard Lipschitz was strapped to a stainless steel autopsy table, sweating profusely, breathing heavily, and shaking his head back and forth. He was trying to say something, but the ball gag in his mouth converted whatever it was into a distorted garble.

"How're we feeling today, Dickie?" Harry asked. He was dressed in green surgical scrubs and black rubber gloves. In his right hand, he held a hypodermic syringe.

"You'll feel a few slight pinches, and then your testicles will go completely numb. He injected a local anesthetic around the patient's genital region and Lipschitz's eyes widened as he squirmed frantically. He was barely able to move, bound with rope as he was, his arms, wrists, and ankles cuffed to the table with heavy leather cuffs.

"Why fight the inevitable, my little piggy? You'll just wear yourself out. Don't worry, I'll be right baaaack," sang an ecstatic Harry as he disappeared into the kitchen. He returned with a bowl of ice cubes, a small propane cook stove, a frying pan and two "testicles" made of chicken hearts. He rubbed the ice over Lipschitz's balls, and in full view of the patient, opened a chrome scalpel from its sterile wrapper and began the fake castration amid Lipschitz's heightened squirming and desperate screams, which stopped abruptly. Richard Lipschitz had passed out.

A few minutes later, Harry waved smelling salts under Dick's nose. He woke to the scent of the chicken hearts being sautéed in the skillet.

"You must be hungry. I think I forgot to feed you yesterday, my little Gomez."

"Aaaaaaarrrrrrrgggggggggghhhhhhhh!!!!!" screamed the victim, around the perimeter of the rubber ball gag. His nostrils flared, eyes wide, like a horrified wild animal.

"Is something wrong?" Prudence stopped reading. Harry was almost fully prone, lying on his back and twitching as though he was having an epileptic fit. Concerned, she reached out to him. "Are you okay?"

Harry abruptly came to and sat up. "Ah, sure. I'm fine. Um, sorry." He grinned.

Prudence, assuming he'd been paying attention, continued with her reading.

"Morgan began his prison term and my life was changed forever. The end."

With her piece finished, they took a break and made some more tea. And then it was Harry's turn.

"Ummmm... This is part of something I've been working on. Sort of a screenplay format. Just finished it yesterday." He looked down at his manuscript and began to read.

Seth waits on the street that evening, knowing that Georgia and Richard are attending an event. He watches them leave and waits for the new doorman to arrive. As a group of gay men enter the building, Seth slips in with them, taking the lift up to the 32nd floor with the group of chuckling, very tipsy guys.

CUT TO:
INT: ELEVATOR
                    GUY ONE *(to Seth)*
Whose little boy are you?

They all laugh...

SETH
(under his breath)

If only you knew....

Seth smiles slightly and nods to his fellow passengers, wondering what it would be like to slash all their throats and simply walk away. He turns his back to them as the door for his floor slides open.

GUY TWO

<u>Our</u> party's in 35L. You're invited. Wear your birthday suit!"

Everyone laughs, except Seth.

Harry took a sip of the herbal tea and continued reading.

INT: GEORGIA'S HALLWAY, NIGHT

Seth has made a copy of the key to the new lock on Georgia's door. He inserts the key and enters. The apartment, once sleek and modern has dramatically changed into a gothic dungeon. Quite different since his last visit a few months ago. This takes his breath away. He sighs, doing some deep breathing. Regaining his composure, he takes a small vial of liquid mushroom extract out of his backpack and opens the refrigerator. A bottle of red wine is right where a succession of bottles has been since Richard showed his miserable face in 32L six months ago. Knowing that Richard only drinks red, he removes the cork and pours the liquid into the bottle. He rummages around, looking in closets, drawers and under the bed, discovering all manner of corsets and toys and straps and ropes and gags. Suddenly, the sound of the two of them laughing outside the door and drunkenly fumbling for keys startles him out of his obsessive searching. He squirms under the bed just as they enter the apartment, laughing and groping each other.

INT. GEORGIA'S LIVING ROOM, NIGHT
GEORGIA
(in her drunken German junkie accent)
I'm going to make you squeal like a little pig tonight.

LIPSCHITZ
(squealing, really getting into it)

• 171 •

Oink, oink, oink.

They both tumble onto the floor, laughing and tearing each other's clothes off. Richard crawls to the fridge a few feet away, opens it and pulls out the bottle of red with one hand. Then returns his other hand to continue doing its work under her skirt. He uncorks the bottle with his giant fake teeth and takes a huge swig, then offers some to her, working the bottle into her mouth like a cock. She plays along, going down on the bottle, then takes a swig herself. They play this game for a while until the last drop is gone.

LIPSCHITZ
That tasted a little moldy. You should check the temperature in your wine cellar.

Harry sat on the couch, reading his script. He was oblivious to Prudence's obvious discomfort. While she listened, her eyes were pinched shut. Bent forward, she cradled the top of her head in her arms. He continued reading:

Both drunk, they laugh convulsively at this stupid joke. Meanwhile, Seth is watching all of this from under the bed. He didn't expect to be there when they returned. He did not want to witness any of this, but now he is stuck, without his video camera or audio recorder. He can only lie there and watch and listen. The debauchery continues in the other room, but in clear view of Seth, eyes wide. Georgia is riding Richard around like a pretend pony. They are both naked except for Richard's black socks, a hole in one heel. Richard's necktie is in his mouth like a horse bit. She is holding the reigns with one hand, and sliding the neck of the bottle in and out of his asshole with the other. Richard groans with pleasure. His gut and man-boobs seem to almost drag on the floor, like a bitch after too many litters.

GEORGIA
(in her German junkie accent)
Is my little pot-bellied piggy happy?

LIPSCHITZ

Yes, Mistress Coco.

His voice is muffled by the tie. As they make their way to the bed, the magic mushroom extract begins to kick in. She feels the effects first as the room softly vibrates and the walls undulate as if under water. The low lights and candles break down into separate colors of the spectrum and begin a slow rhythmic swirl, like dozens of rainbow tornados. She blinks, not believing what she is seeing. She is head down with her butt in the air, knees on the bed. Lipschitz's snout is in her ass, porcine tongue slobbering every which way underneath. His eyes are closed.

CUT TO:
LIPSCHITZ'S POV HALLUCINATIONS

Like a cartoon video football game from the POV of a tight end running with the ball. Seemingly dozens of defensive opponents are charging after him. He narrowly escapes being tackled...then finally getting tackled, flipping up into the air, fumbling the ball...when he....

CUT TO:

...lifts his saliva covered jowls, looking up from Georgia's tight firm ass. There are no cartoons going on in the rest of the room. Lipschitz resembles a hyena tearing into the flesh of a freshly killed wildebeest, with a similar kind of pathological greed, focus and voracity. As his eyes adjust from the total darkness of her ass to the dim swirling light tornados, he gazes dumbly around the room, light rays flitting about.

LIPSCHITZ
Where are we baby?

She dumbly gazes at Richard, not answering, and squirms slightly away. Reaching for the dildo belt, she orders Richard.

GEORGIA
Belly on bed! Face on floor! Open your ass...wide!

He obeys without question. She straps on the belt expertly with one hand; with the other prepares his anal sphincter with a fist full of lube, then rams him, fucking like a little dog. Richard groans. He has been transported to another time and place. His brain is cotton candy. His fat dimpled ass could be a sausage skin stuffed full of large curd cottage cheese. His head and forearms are mashed into the floor by his own mass and from the rapid grinding in his ass by the petite dominatrix-whore above on the bed. His body is tingling with pleasure, but his mind is in a place that it has never been before. He is beginning to peak from the magic mushroom potion. Hallucinating wildly, he opens his eyes slightly, looking upside down under the bed. He sees what looks like a face and a pair of eyes with gold rimmed glasses looking directly at him. He closes his eyes and opens them again. The face remains. He mouths, <u>What the fuck?</u> He tries to talk, but he can't. In fact, he can't even move. Like a mute rag doll being fucked by a crazed tiger-cat, he helplessly looks at the face under the bed, sixteen inches away from his, while the room undulates, changing ever so slowly, elongating and compressing, distorting like a mirrored reflection at a carnival. Lipschitz's breathing speeds. He passes out in a heap on the floor. Georgia crawls off the bed, and with surprising strength hauls her love slave off the floor and back onto the bed, then passes out herself. She is on her back, still wearing the strap on; pink boner pointing straight up. After a beat, Seth, crawls out from underneath the bed and removes the dildo, holding it with a piece of newspaper. He rolls Georgia over on her stomach; sees a black marking pen on the night stand, and writes on her naked ass, "Kilroy was here!!" He walks over to the window and tosses the dildo out into the night. In slow motion, it floats, end over end, thirty-two stories, down toward the street. It lands in a tree, getting caught by the branches, perching like a pink, rubbery bird.

Motionless after hearing this tale of debauchery, Prudence managed to whisper, "Yeah... uh, I gotta go to sleep now. Time for you to leave."

"It's just a story," Harry reassured her.

"Yeah, no problem," she lied, trying to be polite. "It was amazing. Just, ahhh... I am just ahh... a bit tired now. No offense."

"Okay. I'll call you soon then."

Harry silently let himself out. He heard the door locks click and the chain latched as he walked to the elevator.

Chapter 50

Well, so much for Prudence. And all the rest: Dty Barbera, Kathy, Linda, Toni, Deidre, Melissa, Donna, Ausome9, Slightlyexotic, deedee, Flaxwell, Tahinidew, serenashakti, happylg, and sweethart4you44.

The whole dating thing was only for research purposes anyway, he reminded himself. Something for the archive, for the book, or for whatever Harry ended up using his hours of notes and transcripts and surveillance videos. He was on his back, on the couch, twirling his hair, lost in thought, reflecting on those 5,000 pages of emails. All the recorded and carefully transcribed conversations, the newspaper clippings from the fall of The Sanguine Estate and those countless hours of videos and home porn; all that done and gathered while he managed to maintain a completely artificial friendship with Georgia. He knew all about what was going on between Lipschitz and her as a result of his obsessive email hacking, Because of this knowledge, Harry was able to easily creep back into her life during their many conflicts, showing up at just the right time.

Hey old friend can I help out with a chore or two; this way he showed how kind and understanding he could be. Maybe he occasionally cooked dinner, and knowing how much she liked to drink, he bought several bottles of her favorite Chardonnay. On a few such occasions, he even ground up a couple of Ambien tablets and secretly added pinches of the powdered sleeping potion. He watched her pass out and then "helped" her off with her clothing and carried her into the bedroom where he woke her from her Ambien and wine induced coma and she became an encouraging and consenting adult; her guard reduced to nothing. And he could have his way.

His online dating project, as he referred to it, as well as his interest in the relationship between Georgia and Lipschitz, his research, and his spying—all of it, as far as Harry was concerned, was coming to an end.

This magnum opus could use a little more energy, he thought, a conclusion and a dénouement. "A well-documented meeting with me and Lipschitz might make for some interesting drama. Just like a scene out of The Conversation," he said aloud, invoking his favorite movie, "I could get Liv and some others to walk around our public meeting, recording everything secretly. And, of course, I'd have my hidden recorder."

A while later, Harry was still on the couch, lost in thought, working an eyebrow, when the phone rang. It was Liv.

"Harry...touching base my friend...just thinking about you."

"And back at ya, my beloved. I was just thinking about you, too. I have a job for you. I want to set up a meeting with Lipschitz in some public place, like maybe Bryant Park. I was hoping you, and maybe some assistant, might be able to secretly shoot all this...our meeting...you know, stills and video. I'll, of course, be wired for audio... it would be right out of The Conversation...remember...our favorite movie."

"This creeps me out Harry...but, yeah, okay, let's do it," Liv said. "It actually could be fun...life imitating art and all that; okay, I'm there!"

She sounded scared, but excited adding, "And let's hope this is cathartic enough to put an end to your obsession with all this crap. Please promise me that you will stop if I help you."

"Okay, after this I'll stop," he said, knowing he wouldn't. After all, it wasn't finished yet.

A short while later he emailed Georgia.

From: Harry Waldheim@mac.com
To: Georgia Pendleton@gmail.com

Subject: clearing the air

Dear Georgia,

I've been thinking that maybe we ought to clear the air a bit between we three, you, Richard and me. I propose a meeting with Richard sometime in the near future, not to be friends, but maybe to just not be enemies. What's the point, right, life's too short. If you think this makes any sense, please forward this note.

Hugs, -H

Richard took the bait and agreed to meet in Bryant Park, three days later. For their meeting "as gentlemen," Lipschitz showed up fifteen minutes early with his buddy, Frank, the carpenter from The Sanguine Estate, who was there "for protection" and to be a witness if Harry got violent (which was certainly Lipschitz's hope).

"I am going to be as insulting and hostile and accusing and nasty as possible with this guy," he told Frank before the meeting. "I have no doubt that he will try to assault me. That's when you jump in, right? Pull him off me and call the cops. Then we'll get this bastard thrown in jail!"

Frank agreed to the plan. He was, after all, a lot bigger than Harry and knew he could take him. And from what Richard said, the guy was nuts.

Lipshitz sat at the table next to the merry-go-round, where he and Harry agreed to meet, talking on the phone to Georgia.

"As soon as he shows up I'll press the redial button and set my Blackberry on the table on speakerphone. You will be able to hear everything. But, just remember, we can hear you too, so please cover your mouthpiece."

Georgia responded, "You're so clever to think of this. That's why I'm with you and not him. Please be careful. If he gets violent, Frank is there, right?"

"Yep. I can see Frank quite clearly from where I'm sitting. But hold it, I think his pecker is hanging out. I'd better go remind him that he's in a public place."

Georgia laughed, "You are so bad. You're gonna get it tonight. And I'll have all afternoon to think about just what "it" is going to be."

"Promises, promises. Oh, there he is. I'm hanging up, and expect me to push redial in a few minutes. Love ya babe."

He hung up and stood formally, to greet Harry.

Chapter 51

"Hey, it's been a while," Harry said, already wishing he'd prepared a script as he fought back a surge of nausea. Just looking at this vile perv disguised as a prosaic low-level corporate drone almost caused him to retch. He was suddenly overtaken by the memory of being forced to drink sour milk as a child. The sight of those warm bottles sitting in the hallway of the Presley School, warm putrid curd rising to the top. He shook, involuntarily, and then offered Richard a hand.

They shook hands, sizing each other up, like two prize fighters about to begin round one.

"How are you?" asked Lipschitz, with unconvincing confidence.

"I'm good. Were you happy to get out of the office early today? You should thank me for that," poked Harry, getting ready for round one.

Ignoring this bit of small talk, Lipschitz threw the first punch. "What I did was, thinking about the meeting today, put some thoughts down on paper that I think might be a good foundation for us to talk about. So that we can have an open dialogue about what's been going on. The first is a letter I wrote to Violet."

Georgia's shrink, Violet? Harry was caught off guard by this left jab to the body.

"And the second memo is a synopsis of things that were on my mind." A swing and a miss by Lipschitz.

"Wait, are you suggesting that I read this stuff right now?" Harry asked.

Harry noticed Lipschitz's Blackberry was lying flat on the table, red light blinking, and realized that he was either being recorded or was on speaker phone. *Hmmmmm...let me guess, Georgia? This amateur is at least trying to raise the level here.* He thought of the microphone taped to his chest recording their conversation, while his surveillance team cautiously roams the perimeter shooting still and moving images.

"Well gee, I didn't bring my reading glasses. Would you mind reading out loud to me?" It was a long shot, but how cool would it would be to record Little Dickie reading his list? Maybe he could even send a copy to the perv's wife.

"Whatever," declared an exasperated Lipschitz. It was all too obvious he knew Harry would be able to keep dodging his punches. He began to read aloud, as Liv carefully took pictures from a distance.

Dear Violet,

You and I have never met, but you know some things about me already. First, I want to thank you for caring and helping Georgia. She is very important to me and I do love her a lot. Most importantly, however, is her happiness, her professional success, reducing stress in her life, and seeing her smile more. I look to you during this very important time in her life. In my opinion, if she takes on the burden of going to therapy with Harry at this time, it will substantially reduce her ability to concentrate and be successful in her new job, not to mention the cycle of abuse he causes. I have issues with her relationship with Harry, not because I am jealous, but because he is controlling, abusive, and demeaning. I am sure you only know a small percentage of things he has done to her. He met with her parents, against her wishes...

Harry's eyes were closed as he took in all the bullshit. Half listening, he reflected on the day he met up with Georgia's parents.

They were having lunch, talking about the wonderful nine years he gave their daughter. Georgia's mom, June, very pert and perky, was jumpy and animated as she spoke. Her dad, in contrast, was almost stone silent as he quietly downed his second scotch, before the food arrived with a bottle of white wine. Upper middle class WASPs, they fit the mold to a tee.

"Georgia gave us very little pleasure as a child," said June, after a few hearty swigs of Chardonnay.

"Well, I wish I knew how I could get her back. We talked about getting married last summer, and I guess that scared her off. I expected to spend the rest of my life with her," faked-Harry, playing the victim for the somber luncheon audience. Of course, he was recording everything with the hidden microphone in his breast pocket.

"Maybe she runs away from things. Well, I didn't want to say anything, but Georgia's sister told me that she left you six months ago," confided June.

"Huh..."

That lying, sneaking bitch, Harry thought to himself. Out loud he said, "I had no idea." He paused thoughtfully. "Although, I did have my suspicions, way back then, that she was having an affair with her dentist. She used to spend so much time with him. All those late night appointments. And all that money. I think she replaced every single one of her teeth."

"Well, we certainly know about the money," June piped in, "We must have given her over fifty grand and still have not received an accounting from her. We were beginning to wonder what else she spent it on, or if it all went into her mouth."

Harry changed the subject. "You know," he confessed, "I went online, and since we had the same password, I could easily read all of her emails. One of them was from Roz...you know...that woman Georgia always referred to as her Jewish mother...telling Georgia how sick and twisted I was. Further, she complained that we, meaning you two and me, were all stifling her development. This is who is advising her. This surrogate parent is poisoning her mind." He felt obligated to rat out Georgia and get a little revenge.

A waiter interrupted. "Chicken, endive, and shaved fennel..." He put the oversized bowl in front of Georgia's mother, then served her father and finally Harry.

Georgia's mother seemed unsurprised. "I'll say again, we've not had a great deal of pleasure with Georgia. When she was fourteen she became anorexic."

"I had no idea." Harry responded, genuinely surprised.

"Yes, from fourteen until she graduated from college."

"She almost died. She got down to eighty pounds," Georgia's dad, Bart finally added to the conversation.

Her mother interrupted, "That's right, she almost died. And I know for a fact that even though she hardly spoke a word to us until after she graduated from college—during the time she was really sick, I was the scapegoat. I was her target, and she would say terrible things to me using words that she had never used before."

"You never really get over anorexia. There's something in your brain. It's a physical and mental problem," chimed in her newly-awakened dad.

June interrupted again, "I feel that we never regained her. We had three children very close together, and she may have needed more care than we could give her."

Harry snapped back into the present as Lipschitz continued reading:

"...I feel that Harry should be prevented from having any contact with Georgia for at least six months. After all he has done to her, she deserves so much better than he is capable of. I know you and me have the same goal: to see Georgia smile more, have less stress in her life and to have a successful career.

Sincerely,

Richard P. Lipschitz.

"Wow, Dick. You write a mean memo. Really. What's on page two, pray tell?"

Not conceding to the sarcasm, Richard continued. "Well, I have a lot of issues with your behavior. After all you put Georgia and I through, after all you have done to us, she and I are in a very close and committed relationship. Our relationship is personal and private. You don't respect that." Lipschitz sat up straight, thinking he scored some brilliant points.

"That's very true, Dick. Your relationship with her is based on deceiving your wife and children, and me as well. My relationship with Georgia is also personal and private, and has nothing to do with you whatsoever...*comprende?* Where's your respect for my privacy?"

Ignoring Harry's last statement, Lipschitz continued, "I know you are very jealous. And you did some really bad things. You called my house and threatened me and you threatened me to Georgia. You stole our sex toys. Twice! And that's really weird and scary. You really stepped over the line with that one. Lemme finish reading this list, then we can discuss.

Item one: you made Georgia feel scared of you."

Meanwhile, Georgia was listening to the conversation in Bryant Park, on her headset, furiously takes notes. She couldn't help feeling how clever they were to be spying on Harry. She listened as he responded to Richard's prosecution. Of course, she had no clue Harry was recording all of this for his *own* use.

Lipschitz continued, "Item two: You have manipulated her and taken advantage of her kindness. Item three: You called my house. Item four: You threatened me. Item five: You have said derogatory things about me to Georgia. Item six: You stole our sex toys!"

As Lipschitz read, Harry tuned him out and instead examined the man's split nose and stumpy fingers, capped teeth and glued on hair. A black speck fell from the tree above, floating down slowly and landing on his nose. *Man that rug sure looks real*, Harry thought. *I'll have to get the number of his rug guy just in case, god forbid, I get a little thin upstairs myself.*

Out loud, Harry said, "Eh, Dick. You got a little speck there." Harry pointed to his nose, almost touching it, "Yeah, right on the end of your nose. And what's with the scar? It's like the whole length of your nose. What did the other guy look like?"

Lipschitz cocked his head slightly, staring into Harry's eyes.

That was the day he was hit in the face with a board by the captain of his high school wrestling team, four of his teammates held him while Jimmy Murcogliano spat in his face, then slammed his nose, splitting it almost perfectly in half.

"You and your fucking stiff cock, you sick perv, fuck!" the kid had said.

Poor Richard had no control over his frequent sexual arousal during wrestling practice, and as a mere third stringer he rarely had the opportunity to compete. The few times that he did, though, his obvious hard-on not only sickened the audience, but completely skeeved out his opponents, triggering their fight-or-flight reflexes with such strength that Lipschitz would be pinned the instant his opponent felt the rubbery boner sliding against him.

Pretending to ignore Harry's last comment, Lipschitz continued. "Item seven: You broke into her e-mails. Item eight: You disrespected her to her friends. Item nine: You used her parents against her. Item ten: When I wanted to see her after her facelift surgery, you did not let me.

Ah, the facelift, Harry remembered. Georgia was never particularly fond of the way she looked. She convinced her sister to pay for breast implants, her parents to buy her a complete set of capped teeth, and then there was the facelift. Harry was never sure who paid for that, nevertheless, she went ahead with it and convinced Harry to take care of her, staying at his apartment during her two-week recovery. The evening after her surgery, she arrived by taxi with an Irish nurse who sat with her every evening for the next ten days.

As she emerged from the cab, Harry's video camera rolled. Georgia's head was wrapped in thick layers of ace bandages and cotton, showing only her bloodied face; the entirety of her epidermis having been surgically removed—to promote new skin growth, he was told. This was yet another strange and fortuitous bit of Georgia's behavior for him to document. The next two weeks provided Harry with some of his best footage ever.

"Item eleven: You have tried to inject yourself in the project with Mistress Chunxx. Item twelve: You tried to set up an appointment with Mistress Coco over Chunxx's website.

Harry pondered item twelve. This one, at least, had some truth to it. "You know on a scale of one to ten," he began, "this stuff is, like, a minus one. So I was jealous. That's pathetic, no big deal, nothing more. It's not like I have some kind of strategy here," he lied.

"You know, when she was staying with me, recovering from her facelift," he teased, "she told me she wanted to get back together."

For an instant he returned to that moment, in which Georgia felt genuinely close to him. "I want to be together with you forever. I want us to have our relationship back. I love you," Georgia had said. Her head was still wrapped in gauze bandages. Her face was covered with stitches and caked in dried blood. Harry smiled and kissed her hand as he applied Vaseline to her wounds with a Q-tip.

"I love you too. So happy you're with me," he replied. And he was telling the truth. They both were. Her vulnerability and his being able to care for her in this weakened condition aroused and opened his heart. She was a stray animal, run over by a truck, and Harry was nursing her back to health. She was totally dependent on him, and he rose to the occasion. All with the added bonus of driving Lipschitz crazy. Harry had never been happier, recording every moment of this for the archive.

"You know, I spent a year and a half hoping that she would come back to me," Harry explained to Lipchitz. "And then she did. And then she reneged. And now here we are, you and me. What do you expect from Georgia? Friendship? Lovers? Platonic? What?"

"I think you're getting into the personal aspect of my relationship with her, which is something I am not willing to continue to talk about." stated Lipschitz, attempting to control the situation.

"So, you're pleading the fifth?"

"I'm just saying that's personal. What's important to me is Georgia's happiness," Lipshitz added, remembering she was listening in on the conversation.

Harry shook his head in disagreement. "Well, she hasn't been too terribly happy since she got involved with you, the past year and a half."

"We've had some wonderful moments together. She's a great lady."

"Oh, great lady. Now there's a term. What year were you born, again?" Harry gaped in disbelief, wondering what Georgia could possibly see in this moron?

"You know there's a certain kind of immediate gratification in your relationship with Georgia. Like entertainment and recreation, just having fun. Everybody needs fun, right? She went for you in a spontaneous and impulsive way, and to her credit, she had an adventure. And for that, I respect her."

Lipshitz realized he'd lost control of the conversation and butted back in. "Let's get back to the subject of the inappropriate stuff you did and said to Georgia," he spat.

Harry ignored him, and pressed on. "Do you define betraying your family as appropriate or inappropriate?"

"My family is not part of this conversation!"

"But you are being dishonest and disrespectful and expecting me to live up to a higher standard than you ever could," responded Harry, goading. "And...Georgia is my family."

"She's not your family."

"She is to me."

"You're not married."

"So?"

"She's not your family."

"So, you're married, yet you betray your family. Help me out here with your definition of what a family is?"

Lipschitz, exasperated, whined, "I said we're not talking about my family. If you have any questions about Georgia, fine. Otherwise we're finished here. Give Georgia her space and help her out, or stay away. Full stop!"

"Okay tough guy. But, I actually do help her. Didn't she tell you? The other day she asked me to help her with her website, so I shot some video and some stills. I even bought her a little vinyl nurse's outfit."

Georgia stood still as a mannequin, in Harry's apartment, as he wrapped her naked body with strips of silk and leather ribbon. His nimble fingers pulled bits of fabric over her shoulders, crisscrossing her back, wrapping around her front to the sides of her ridged silicone breasts. He lingered for a second, his forefinger barely grazing an erect nipple, before the tip of his tongue flicked a lick. He looked up for encouragement only to receive a very stern, dominatrix look back, that told him, in no uncertain terms, he should cease and desist. Harry obeyed, retracting his horny tongue, and continued the work of dressing her for the photo shoot in his makeshift studio. A roll of white, seamless paper was the only backdrop. Two soft boxes, the only lighting. A video camera on a tripod recorded all the movement while Harry prepared Georgia. He wrapped an intricate maze of fabric and leather strips around her waist and then separated the cheeks of her firm slender buttocks, exposing the well-manicured pink star. He gazed longingly at the prize, inhaling its subtle musk, which somehow penetrated his blood-insect-brain barrier. Harry shuddered with lust, yet continued to play by the rules. No more subtle flicks of fingers nor of tongue; he kept working on Georgia's outfit.

Then, camera in hand, eye at the lens, he dove into another world—one that only existed through a lens—each shot framed with passion and expertise, clear and crisp images in rapid succession, isolated and focused, highly charged and very much alive.

Georgia was absolutely uninhibited, a full-fledged exhibitionist. Harry felt the control she had in teasing his cock. She remained cold and distant, hating the camera—and maybe the photographer, as well, but who cared. This was yet more crazy shit for the archive.

Lipschitz noticed Harry off on a daydream, and tried to draw him back. "I've written down some of the bad things that you did, and based on that I counseled Georgia to stay away from you. I understand you love this woman and she left you. And she left you in a way that..."

"Yes," Harry interrupted, "and then she came back to me and then left and then came back again."

"Did you know that we were dating when you went away with her on New Year's?" asked the perplexed and bruised Lipschitz.

New Year's eve was the last time that Harry and Georgia were together at *Wonderhouse*, a name they'd fondly given the old farmhouse Harry purchased several relationships prior. They would sometimes spend weeks at a time together there, she gardening and taking naked photographs of herself. The mossy woods filled with old growth hemlocks and sugar maples were perfect for such sport. Patches of bright green ferns crowded numerous giant boulders, dropped randomly by glaciers twenty thousand years ago. Shy hermit thrushes filled the air with their lonely, bubbling chorus of pan pipes. He did endless chores, tinkering and repairing around the old house; pushing a rock up a hill, he'd often say.

Those were peaceful times—times when they felt the closest, perhaps loving the house more than each other. Georgia still felt attracted to something there, and was easily convinced to spend one last New Year's eve together.

Besides, Lipschitz had family obligations, with the holidays going on, and had little choice but to maintain his family man subterfuge. Or maybe it really was his preference, and Georgia was only the trophy WASP on the back burner. No matter. She hadn't wanted to be alone then, and decided to be with Harry at the sacred and tranquil farmhouse one last time.

Be prepared Harry had learned as a young Eagle Scout. Yet who could have predicted that his past training would ever bring him to this point? He packed both video and audio recorders, four bottles of Chardonnay, one liter of the best Russian vodka he could find, one bottle of absinthe and thirty Ambien tablets. Not that he needed more than a couple secretly dissolved into a shot of vodka or glass of Chardonnay to get Georgia in the mood. At last he'd found a source of the elusive *Spanish fly*, something he'd read about at age ten. After all these years, he discovered a combination of alcohol and Ambien did the trick.

After a late afternoon walk along the freshly plowed country road, they settled in on a futon placed in front of the old stone fireplace. Well-dried sugar maple logs crackled, filling the house with aromatic, sensual warmth. Off to the side sat a gym bag, containing a small riding crop, a dildo, and a tiny vibrator, just in case. Georgia emerged, freshly washed, from a hot shower, her hair wet and combed back, wrapped in a long white towel. She accepted a glass of doctored Chardonnay from Harry, who had just turned on the hidden camera.

She lounged on the futon, her legs modestly folded to one side, absent-mindedly combing her hair, drying it by the heat of the fire. The only source of light in the room, the flames pulsed in random surges of amber and orange as they popped and crackled.

She looked so damn sexy sitting there, Harry thought. He prepared their feast of simple, poached salmon, steamed asparagus, a salad consisting of endive, arugula, shaved cauliflower, persimmon and pomegranate, and for dessert, red raspberries with lemon sorbet, and of course, plenty to drink. He even brought a couple of hits of pot—again, just in case. Be prepared.

They ate and drank, sitting in front of the fire, a slow, steady crescendo of lust gaining momentum. Soon he was on his back, head in her lap. Still wrapped in a towel, hair mostly dry, she opened his mouth, dropping a single red raspberry past lips and teeth, hitting his tongue. He cleverly pushed another berry back out on the end of his tongue. "It's for you," he said. Taking the bait, she bobbed down, removing it with her thin, delicate lips. She pushed it back into Harry's mouth with a strong and determined tongue. They played this game and were soon naked and hot on the futon, the eroticism of the embers warming and encouraging them. She was reeling, and horny from the Ambien cocktail.

They took their time, teasing and fucking, kissing and licking, and fucking some more, then withdrawing again, more drinking, a hit of pot, more kissing and licking. And then, then Harry whispered, "Could you tie me up? Could you dominate me and whip me, Mistress?"

How many times, before he asked this question, had he imagined her enthusiastic response. He envisioned them in love and Lipschitz gone forever. But, like a plug, suddenly yanked from its outlet, she laid a sudden slap on his face: a sucker punch from nowhere, an assassin's bullet. The warm and loving room turned to ice. Georgia sat up, turning her back to him.

"That is really manipulative! Don't ever ask me to do that again!" She lit a cigarette and swigged directly from a nearby bottle of vodka.

"What the fuck?" Harry withdrew immediately, hurt and bruised. "What did I say?" he wondered. She was a friggin' dominatrix. He'd thought she'd enjoy his submission. But for Georgia, this was different. Gomez and only Gomez was her submissive, along with paying clients, of course. To cross over, to bring Harry into her sacred world of sadism and masochism and bondage and discipline was unthinkable; an invasion of her autonomy, of a private affair that she and only she could control.

Five minutes later, with another doctored Chardonnay, a cigarette, and a cup of chamomile tea for Harry, they reconvened in front of the fire. His cock was still hard from hours of teasing. "I'm sorry," he lied, hoping to at least complete his sexual conquest. Georgia, having roughly the same thought, and still being aroused herself, set down the mostly-empty wine glass. Then, ever so professionally, wrapping thumb and fore-finger around the base of Harry's engorged cock, she began licking it del-icately around the rim of its purple head, and then inside the tiny horizontal smile. And then, like a sword swallower, she took it all the way down. They were back at it, and the game continued on and on into the night.

The next morning, a winter chill filled the creaky wooden house, which had never been properly insulated. Harry and Georgia were tucked under a warm down comforter on the futon, insulating them from the morning chill. First up, a naked Harry rekindled the fire, checked his recording devices, dressed, and made coffee and French toast.

"I need to use your car," declared Georgia, breaking her hung over silence. She sat at the kitchen table in sweat pants and Harry's old buffalo plaid flannel shirt, drinking her coffee and ignoring her French toast. She gazed out the window at the white expanse of the freshly blanketed field, squinting into the bright sun.

"Of course," agreed Harry. "Just let me grab a couple of things out of it, and it's all yours."

This was perfect, he thought. She had to check in with her beloved pot-bellied pig. While Georgia prepared for her drive, Harry put a charged battery and a new memory card into his tiny audio recorder and slipped it under the front seat, strategically placing the mic. He pushed record.

"What are you doing?" asked Georgia.

Startled by her appearance, Harry blurted out, "Ahahh....just warm-ing her up for you." She jumped in and peeled out, setting out to the closest spot that, for no particular reason, received a mobile phone signal. Harry figured there must have been at least fifty calls from her beloved Gomez, by that time.

Later, when Harry went back to the recording, he heard Georgia calm-ing her frantic, jealous, love slave, "I miss you too... Oh...nothing much...a very boring night, but at least quiet and peaceful. What time can we meet tomorrow? Good.... You'd better be wearing my underwear and keeping that rubber ding-dong where I put it the other night." She laughed in response to something unintelligible. And then finally, "To-morrow... We are going to make some L-O-V-E" she proclaimed with authority.

Back in Bryant Park, Lipschitz, snapped his fingers in Harry's face. "Hello..."

Finally, Harry returned to the here and now. "You know, I have no respect for your relationship with her. It's an adulterous relationship that's based on betrayal. So, I have a real problem with that."

"Well, now you're getting all moral here."

"The issue is not morals, but rather ethics," declared Harry.

"Ethics?" responded Lipschitz, as though that was a word he'd never, ever encountered.

"If you're, at one point, telling someone to be trustworthy and honest and straightforward, and then, on the other hand, you're betraying other people... Not just other people, but this family that you supposedly have such high regard for, *your* family, then you are in no position to point the finger at me or anybody else. He who lives in a glass house, etcetera, catch my drift?" lectured Harry, feeling smug about scoring the point.

Lipschitz attempted to con for an ounce of sympathy and pretended to agree. "Yeah, no... absolutely... I'm just at a point in my life... you know... emotionally I'm on a roller coaster ride with all this. My relationship with Georgia is the honest relationship. I don't have that with my family. I would be bullshitting you if I told you I did. Believe it or not, I've never lied to Georgia. That's the truth."

"Are you going to fuck her when you go on your rafting trip this weekend?" Harry asked, going on the offensive.

"That's none of your business. I have never fucked her. I don't fuck, I make love."

"What are your romantic expectations for this trip? Will you try to seduce her? I know you are a very persuasive, seductive, sales-pitch kind of guy," Harry taunted.

"I have never seduced her or attempted to sell her on me. End of conversation. You're jealous... admit it." Lipschitz, was on the offensive now, knowing his buddy Frank was nearby to pull Harry off of him and call the cops should he get physical. Then Harry could be arrested for assault.

"Absolutely. Jealousy is a horrible prison for a person, as is anger and rage. Some people go absolutely nuts in this kind of situation. I'm not exactly proud of the way I acted, or of the thoughts that I had. But nobody got hurt... not even close. And, my dear friend, all of your information about me is secondhand hyperbole, which adds up to misinformation. It's very easy to spin this into *Harry is psycho*."

"Well, that's the way it was represented to me—you *are* a psycho."

"So, that's what you want to believe. Maybe you watch too much television. Or maybe you feel so guilty about being a schmuck that you secretly want Freddy Kruger to jump out of the bushes and fuck you up," added Harry, sarcastically.

"Whatever. I think we accomplished all that we could today," Lipschitz pronounced as he got up to leave, clearly exasperated. He glanced over at Frank sitting at a nearby table pretending to read the paper, and gave him the nod—it was time to go.

Harry remained seated watching his mortal enemy disappear into a crowded Bryant Park, then called Liv on her mobile.

"Liv, where are you?"

"I'm right here. I can see you. I'll wave. Turn to your right ninety degrees."

"Did you get any good shots? How many did you take? I didn't notice you once. I thought maybe you chickened out. Man was that guy disgusting."

"Yeah, I know, I saw him," Liv responded. "Gaaah!"

"I only wish I'd asked him what he had up his ass today. Are you wearing Georgia's underwear? Are those clothespins on your balls giving you any discomfort today? When the movie comes out we'll do a reenactment, where you have an X-ray camera pointed to the side of his ass, so you can see what's in there. I want to destroy this bastard. I don't care what happens to me. I'm bringing every bit of evidence I own to his wife."

Harry glanced toward the merry-go-round and watched the children spin around, laughing and having fun.

Then he noticed a young boy, blond, holding on to an upright brass pole, staring straight ahead. Their eyes met. It was young Harry, at age eight. He looked away, and when he looked back again, the child was gone.

Liv arrived and sat next to Harry. She lovingly put her arm around him and he slumped into her, totally lost.

Chapter 52

Several weeks after meeting Richard Lipschitz face-to-face in Bryant Park, having looked into the soulless dead-fish eyes of his mortal enemy, and having, in his mind, torn his adversary to shreds, Harry remained isolated in the comfort and seclusion of his apartment. This was his sanctuary, surrounded by books and music, not to mention a vast archive of surveillance media, the result of two years of obsessive stalking, spying and manipulation. But to what end, he wondered.

Harry began the daunting task of organizing hundreds of hours of audio recordings and transcripts, digitizing countless video tapes, filing thousands of emails printed out with great care and obsession. He organized them by category: perv notes, love notes, the rise and fall of The Sanguine Estate, dog running, et cetera.

He combed through Mistress Chunxx's website, downloading video clips of her and Georgia torturing fat, middle-aged men in curly blonde wigs, wearing pink lace panties, dark barbs of hair covering arms, legs and backs. These were not attractive people; unloved, un-nurtured, unsatis-fied from birth, they had to grasp for any shred of attention. Affection, for them, was a smash in the face, a fist up the ass, a punch to the solar plexus, a cigarette extinguished on a tongue. Bound, gagged, mummified and humiliated, so that they could be, if only for a moment, delivered from the numbness of their zombie existence.

Who was this woman—his girlfriend of eight years—clad in the most ridiculous costumes of black leather, lace, and vinyl, bleached blonde skag hair, collagen, Botox, and silicone? An anorexic skeleton obediently following the orders of her obese, sadistic guru—smacking around pathetic, grotesque, masochists. *Who was this woman?* He had no idea. The more information he gathered, the less he seemed to know her and the stranger she had become. And this man, this Richard Lipschitz was his polar opposite: vile, prosaic, corporate, voracious, greedy, deceiving father, Jewish victim, playing every card, every angle, every scheme, con man, lost soul. But was he really so different from Harry? Was it their very similarities that Harry hated most about this man?

As he continued organizing the archive, he came across his file folder of notes and stories, scribbles and thoughts about what to do with this, his tangle of raving, obsessive mania. What am I doing? he wondered, confused, as he began reading.

How I managed to figure out her password and log into her new e-mail account must have had more to do with predestination, certainly, than any ability on my end, other than, perhaps, blind luck and intuition.

"Well, I'll never be a writer, " he mused, collapsing on his back into the comfort and safety of the long couch separating his living area from his desk and tables. All around him, every horizontal surface was covered with file folders, papers, video tapes, and surveillance equipment—the cluttered residue of the last two years. He remembered how often he sat at his editing workstation, combing through hours of secretly recorded videos: Georgia and her man walking arm and arm, toasting each other in fancy restaurants, covered in sweat and booze, drunkenly making out in some smoke filled dive bar, drinking shot after shot.

He remembered his weekly visits to the local underground pistol shooting range, standing cop style, hitting clusters of bulls eyes; his instructor thinking he must be a natural or... special forces, perhaps. He dreamed of his knife collection, for years only consisting of the most ordinary kitchen assortment, now expanded into hunting and commando military daggers, sharpened on both sides, serrated and barbed for maximum effect... he used to obsessively sharpen, and oil them. They were all locked away with his antique gun collection, in the safe, out of harm's way.

He continued reading his journal.

Together they showed me the way of their crimes and led me to the scene, as if it were something that they wanted me to know about—encouraging me to become part of their secret life. I began to feel that this was their plan—to play with my feelings and emotions. Those in the sadomasochist world will openly acknowledge that mind games are a regular part of their diet, after all.

Sometimes I would read about a tryst in their emails, and show up with my camera to tape them talking and dining, drinking wine and toasting to their crimes and to each other. I would spend hours waiting, sometimes shivering on cold winter nights, hiding in some doorway for the perfect moment to press the record button; not unlike an assassin. Gotcha, Lippy!

My guts would burn with rage every time, every limb blown off by a land mine. Not feeling the limb, but terrified by its hideous absence. Georgia was gone, yet there she was, big as life, happily fraternizing with the enemy.

Harry remembered the many times he sat in the dark, freezing in his car; video camera pointed toward two people sitting in the window of a particular favorite West Village French restaurant, sometimes standing in the shadows of doorways, away from street lights, camera in hand; always shivering, anxious, nervous and cold; often apoplectic with rage...

For close to two years I hacked and spied and stalked. Then a miracle happened: she told me she wanted to return to our old relationship. I knew that this was impossible—all the lies and betrayal and her new secret life that I knew all about, unbeknownst to her. But, I played along and even convinced myself that this would work. It lasted close to a week.

Harry still lay on his back, on his couch, safe and comfortable. He stopped reading briefly remembering the time when Georgia was in his bed. Her head was wrapped in bandages and her exposed face was covered with red ooze and stitches after her facelift. He was holding her hand, kissing it, smiling and laughing. He felt absolute joy at her asking to come back; perhaps the past was only a bad dream...then she once again rejected him.

The pain began all over again, spreading through my body almost like the Demerol I injected in the 70's, except with the opposite result. Instead of feeling no pain, the jealous rage returned, the holes in my guts reopened, the childhood memories of bullies and revenge and being invisible came alive again, and with this, the conviction that never again would it happen to me. I went back on line with a vengeance.

Then he remembered the fateful phone call, "You had no right spying on Richard and me... those photographs were our private property... and you have to return those dildos you stole... immediately!" Georgia screamed into the phone.

Harry sat at home, looking over his surveillance video archive and his recently acquired photos. He placed the phone on his desk, in speaker-mode. It was only a week since Georgia left his care and was now on her own, with only a few scabs and pink scars behind her ears and along her jawbone. The one on the back of her neck was already covered in a light down of hair growing nicely back in. He'd spent the previous night at Georgia's: a simple and relaxed evening watching TV and having very gentle and loving sex. As usual she fell asleep way before Harry was even remotely tired, and, with nothing of his own to read, he got up to snoop, an activity he'd begun shortly after he discovered Lipschitz.

He thought he might as well look at Georgia's new headshots. She was always having him shoot the progress of her facelift, and tonight she'd asked him yet again. He complied, but had never had a chance to view the results. Harry lifted the camera up, switched the lever to on, then hit the review button...and there they were, ten photographs; nothing exceptional, not his best work, but a record of Georgia's healing face, none-the-less. He hit the reverse button. What else is here, he wondered. His eyes almost popped out of their sockets, as the next dozen pictures, taken only the day before, revealed Richard Lipschitz being bound, gagged, whipped, beaten and humiliated, by both Georgia and Mistress Chunxx. A giant tooth filled smile on the amused and ecstatic face of Lipschitz revealed the ecstasy of a rocket propelled child, joy-riding in Disney Land, for the first time.

Harry immediately copied the entire contents of her camera memory card to his laptop computer, just in case he missed something, then continued to snoop.

Carefully and quietly, he opened every drawer, meticulously looking under papers and clothing; feeling around with his long fingers, now eying a small, antique, mirrored end table; the one he gave her years ago. He slid the first drawer open.

There they were... practically in broad daylight, not even hidden really, staring back at him with matched intensity: the two dark rubber dildos, fraternal twins perhaps, well used, looking a bit worn even, nesting side by side. They had been conveniently placed in the top drawer, right next to Georgia's bed. How efficient, he thought. Harry carefully removed the twins and silently slid the drawer closed. He placed them in his knapsack, and left a note on the top of the table:

"*Darling, couldn't sleep...what else is new...so, heading back to Harry-land. Love, H*"

Chapter 53

Harry Waldheim's journal

I am now back online with a vengeance. Georgia changed her mind yet again and chose Lipschitz over me. There has never, on the face of this earth, lived or breathed, a creature so void of awareness as Richard P. Lipschitz. His face, his nose split in half, his stumpy fingers, his fake hair, his business casual ensemble; the things he says; his accusations; his self-righteous hypocrisy, his thoughts on family; his fucking bad taste…You vile scum!!! I will rip you to shreds and feed you to your fucking family!! Or, better yet, I will destroy your life, one molecule at a time. You are my new career. Thank you! Now my life is filled with meaning. Klausse2012 is born!!

Be close to your friends and closer to your enemies; that was either Napoleon or Machiavelli. Whateverrrrr….

Chapter 54

Having meticulously sifted through every microscopic bit of e-mail minutia, Harry uncovered clues, tiny insights into Georgia's life. A PayPal notice that could've simply been junk mail turned into an outstanding lead. Georgia had been advertising her services online and had been receiving payments via PayPal under the name Chelsea Chris. Harry discovered a new address: sophisticateNY@gmail.com, and immediately sent an e-mail requesting services using his new address, klausse2012@gmail.com. They began a correspondence.

From: KLAUSSE2012@gmail.com
To: sophisticateNY@gmail.com
Subject: An inquiry

Hello mistress, may I book a session with you? I believe we should meet first, as we have never worked together, and then make the appointment. Can I send you a pic? Monday late afternoon would be good for a pre-session meeting if that works for you. Hope it does,

Klausse.

From: sophisticateNY@gmail.com
To: KLAUSSE2012
Subject: An inquiry

Klausse:

How did you find me? Where are you located? Yes you can send a pic and a little more information as to your experience and interests. Also, can you afford my fee?

From: KLAUSSE2012@gmail.com
To: sophisticateNY@gmail.com
Subject: An inquiry

Dear Mistress,

Well, I've attached a photo....

"Here's his picture." Georgia handed the print out to Lipschitz, who was recently back from yet another job interview. His jacket was neatly hung on the back of a chair. He wore a crisp white shirt, yellow necktie loosened, and was lying on her couch, shoes off, feet up. He studied the photograph as though he were an authority on reading faces.

"This is a strange guy," he noted, with confidence. "Look at his eyes, and fake smile." (The photograph was actually a headshot of Harry's actor friend, Ryan, who agreed, for a small fee, to meet with Georgia and pose as Klausse2012.)

She read aloud:

I don't always have a beard. I've grown it for a play I'm in. As for how I found you; I promised not to divulge my source. I'm sure you understand. I have to admit that I don't have a whole lot of experience with the fetish world. Only dreams and a few training sessions a couple of years ago. But, I am a very willing student and a quick learner. I am certain that I need to do this at this point in my life. I simply can't deal with vanilla any longer. It's just not who I am or ever was, really. Maybe you could help me figure out my likes and dislikes. This I know: I love to watch and am highly voyeuristic. I would love to worship your feet and ass and pussy with my tongue."

Lipschitz slowly shook his head and rolled his eyes, more out of jealousy than anything else. "This guy's a bigger perv than me."

Georgia continued reading.

"I have never had a golden shower, but the idea makes me very hot. Being tied up, especially my cock and balls, could be really great if it was done correctly."

Also, I would like to have my ass trained. Perhaps you could help me with that. Another of my fantasies is that I have this teddy bear that I like to hold while I'm watching. Sort of like we are both watching together. I may also wish not to talk during our sessions and may even want to dress differently when I show up. I enjoy having different identities. Must be the actor in me. I might wear something outlandish under my street clothes and I may or may not want to fully disrobe or remain completely dressed and just listen to you tell me what you'd like me to do—or us do. There are so many possibilities.

If we work well together, I would like this to become a regular thing. Also, I live in Manhattan with my girlfriend, who must never find out about this. Also, also, I am not sure what you might charge me for an hour session. I look forward to our pre-session meeting.

"I hate this guy," grumbled Richard, now seriously jealous, "you can't do this."

"Well, what's the harm in meeting him, It'll be in a totally public and safe place. It's just a meeting, Richard." Georgia was turned on by the strangeness of klausse2012, and she actually liked his face. Secretly, she wondered what a beard would feel like.

Harry was in a costume shop buying an expensive, professionally made false nose, mustache, and goatee, along with theatrical makeup. He tried several different appliances before choosing the right one, and then he tried on several outfits, pawing through piles of shirts, jackets, pants and shoes. When he got home, he sat down at a mirror and carefully applied the nose and make up, adding the mustache and hair.

Arrangements were made for a preliminary meeting between Georgia and Klausse2012. Harry and Ryan met in Madison Park to go over everything, then Ryan got wired with a radio mic.

"Okay Ryan, you got it? I'll be listening in, recording everything. Just be cool and do it like we rehearsed it," coached Harry. "I've hidden a video camera and will be shooting the meeting while in disguise."

Georgia was already there, sitting and drinking a coffee at the agreed upon meeting place, a Starbucks away from her neighborhood. She stood as Ryan approached her and shook his hand. The camera caught her excitement and nerves, as she faked self-confidence.

"Hi. I'm Mistress Chris."

"Hi, I'm Klausse2012. Please call me Klaus."

"Well, first I want to set the ground rules." She looked down at the list that Lipschitz prepared for her, and read:

No drugs or heavy drinking

I will respect your limits, you respect mine

If you own your own toys you can bring them

We will only play safely. I will decide what is safe. I need to know what your experience is, your fantasies, and describe your best sessions. Wearing a mask and being a silent submissive is fine, as you've requested.

Ryan nodded, agreeing with all the ground rules. "Sounds fine to me. Let's take this one step at a time and move forward slowly." He was getting into the role, thinking that maybe being bound and gagged and tied up actually might be fun, even though he was only Harry's proxy. And Georgia, coquette that she was, gave him a jolt of excitement.

"So," she gushed, "I think we could work something out here. Your letter was a tiny bit over the top, but now that I've met you, I think we can begin with some of the basics. You are a voyeur and I'm an exhibitionist. Let's begin there. You will see how uninhibited I am. But be warned. We have to be very clear. No touching, no sex. This is technically a consulting session, if anyone should ask. Now that will be one fifty cash for today's session. See you in two days, 2 p.m. at this address." She handed him her business card:

Mistress Chris

1011 Park Avenue
Apartment 34L
New York City

I'll never tell Richard about any of this, Georgia thought. It could be fun and what he doesn't know won't hurt him.

Two days later, Harry, the real Klause2012, rode up in the elevator holding a teddy bear in front of him. Inside the bear, a small video camera was already silently recording. Just as the door on the 34th floor slid open, he slipped on a cheap, plastic, yellow, smiley-face mask. His murky reflection in the metal elevator doors, while quite creepy, was unrecognizable. He walked down the long sterile hallway, around the corner to 34L, where the door stood slightly ajar. Harry opened it further. Georgia stood, arms folded, bullwhip in hand, wearing thigh-high stilettos, black lace, see-through panties, and a matching see-through corset top.

Georgia was anorexic, almost skeletal—there was not one ounce of body fat on her tiny frame except for her perfectly round, fake boobs. Her recently lifted face looked like some Upper East Side dowager, kind of Nancy Reaganesque. The skin was pulled extremely taut over her protruding chin, her lips burst with collagen, and one eyelid drooped ever so slightly, giving her a bit of an inebriated, embalmed look. Her hair was no longer prim and proper, as it had been in her WASPy realtor past, but now bleached and matted ala Phyllis Diller. Georgia had become a scary, drunken, chain-smoking hag. Harry was taken aback; horrified actually. This was the end for him.

"I can't do this, sorry." He turned on his heels and quickly walked away.

"Harry? What the fuck?!"

Once in the elevator, a mother and her little boy looked down and away from the strangely dressed man. He stared at the kid, and again, suddenly, it was his eight-year-old self. The boy looked up and they stared at one another for what seemed like an eternity as the elevator ever so slowly delivered them down to the lobby.

Chapter 55

The next day, Harry and Dr. Gladstone sat in silence for several minutes. Finally, Gladstone spoke. "This is a pattern you need to break. Let me make a suggestion about what else to do. I want you to close your eyes for a second and take some breaths—slow, even, gentle breaths. There is a part of you that is very young. A part of you that does not want to be abused, a part that is also needy. I'd like you to find that part inside and get an image of him. The young version of you, who wants to feel better. When you have an image of that part, let me know.

"That's easy," Harry said.

"Okay, how old is he?"

"Eight years old."

"What I'd like you to do is take him and put him outside of you for a little while, on either your right side or left side, and put your arm around him."

"Okay."

"Which side is he on?"

"My right side."

"Okay. When he's outside of you, his feelings are outside of you, and you can be an adult for him and be there for him and give him what he never got. So, I'd like you to reassure him that you do love him and that you are going to be there for him and that he's not alone. Whether he believes you or not, at least try to reassure him of that. How's he doing?"

"He's fine. He's calm. I know this little guy," Harry answers, really feeling the presence of the child.

"I believe you, but I'd like you to nurture him in a way that he has never been nurtured before. And one of the best ways I know is to have him outside of you for a short time each day. Let him know that he will be safe. That he will evolve and grow up and he will be okay. You are actually here from his future. You are actually living proof that he grows up. That he will be able to handle life. And, that he can count on you."

The two men sat in silence as Harry quietly wept for this small child, always vulnerable, never protected, tortured, abused—an innocent creature so alone in this cruel world.

"Are you willing to spend some time each day doing that with him in this manner, putting him outside?" asked Gladstone.

"Yes."

"Thank you. Make a promise to him that you will do that, because when you make a promise to a child, you have to keep it. Give him a really big warm hug. Tell him you love him, and that innately, he is just fine. There is nothing wrong with him."

"I did," answered Harry as tears rolled down his face.

"Now you are going to take him back inside. Take a few moments. Take a little while to feel the healing. Sometimes you'll feel it is a pleasing sensation, other times you'll know internally that something has shifted. Whenever you are ready, come back to reality."

"Thanks," whispered Harry.

"You're welcome. It's been my experience, over the years, that the greatest healing comes from self-love."

Chapter 56

Harry loaded a cardboard box with all the papers, photographs, DVDs, newspaper clippings, video tapes and e-mails from his past two years of spying, tailing, following, tracking, tricking, manipulating, stalking and surveilling. He could barely lift it. *Eighty pounds*, he estimated. A hunting knife with a ten inch carbon steel blade, obsessively sharpened and oiled, and an old World War II German Lugar, the one he stole from his grandfather when he was twelve and the old man was on his deathbed.

Harry had rummaged through the attic and basement looking for treasures, and finally found a few—the Lugar and a stash of Nazi pornography, showing pyramids of naked Aryan youth. Teenagers with slender hard-ons in the mouths of nymphets. Pert little breasts at attention. The porn had been long since traded for other porn, but the Lugar sat next to the antique hunting knife on his desk, waiting to be packed into the archive of Georgia and Lipschitz.

"Liv...." Harry had been hoping to actually speak with his beloved best friend, possibly to say goodbye forever, or at least share with somebody what he was about to do. But he got her voicemail, instead. "I had an epiphany..." He left a short message, hung up, and finished packing.

He was on his way to Bucksport, Connecticut from lower Manhattan, through streets clogged with aggressive taxis, bicyclists and pedestrians. His twenty-year-old Ford pickup truck looked out of place but the world was indifferent and unaware of Harry on a mission. Traffic on the West Side Highway was jammed up as usual. No matter, he thought, as he conjured one of his fondest memories of he and Georgia fondling one another—he driving, she a passenger, removing her seatbelt as they headed up into the mountains on the way to Wonderhouse.

He expertly opened her pants with his one free hand, then slid it down the front. She sucked in her firm belly, allowing his large fingers to find their home over the brittle fur, the fuzzy pudendum in need of a shave. Then it was off with her trousers and she was bottomless on her tummy, unfastening his belt, sliding open his zipper, exposing him, rock hard. A lick and a caress, then chugged to the hilt, his right hand pressed firmly down her backside, thumb and forefinger working together, pried apart two firm cloves. The other fingers knew exactly what to do. Meanwhile, still driving seventy miles an hour up the mountainside, with his left hand on the wheel, concentrating on the road, he blasted his hot load.

Good times, good times, he thought.

By then he'd made his way out of Manhattan and was in the Bronx, heading toward the Hutchinson Parkway. The dense traffic had subsided as he glanced down at the Lugar and the hunting knife and the eighty-pound cardboard box. He accelerated with determination, passing a row of several cars—Westchester County Volvos, Mercedes and Audis. The four barrel carburetor of his well-tuned old Ford kicked in, speeding him faster toward the Merritt Parkway.

Deep in the woods, a good distance from the house where he lived with his mother, father and baby brother, eight-year-old Harry stood, watching the flames as they licked into his carefully constructed tree house. He watched as it caught fire—sticks and twigs and leaves and any scrap he could salvage or steal. A bowerbird nest, filled with found treasures. Someone had alerted the fire department, and the sound of the sirens was getting closer. As he stood, watching the flames, a group of volunteer firefighters stumbled toward the scene in their bulky gear. They carried shovels and fire rakes and backpack fire extinguishers.

One of them approached Harry. "What are you doing here, kid?"

Harry just stared silently ahead, ignoring him. He asked again, "I'm talking to you. Did you start this fire? Answer me, you punk."

Harry maintained his silent stare. The firefighter threw his shovel down, grabbed him by the collar and lifted him off his feet, up in the air, pulling him toward his face.

"I don't like you, and you are now in serious trouble boy. Now, what do you know about this fire?"

Instinctively, Harry raised his knees and arms and pushed backward and away from his captor. The man tripped over his unwieldy hip boots and the bulky weight of the fire extinguisher on his back and fell to the ground. All he had of Harry was the boy's shirt collar, which had ripped off in the tussle. As the firefighter struggled to get up, Harry disappeared into the bushes. In the meantime, a group of neighborhood kids gathered around to watch the fire.

The humiliated hero screamed, like a drill sergeant, toward the wide-eyed group of onlookers, "Who was that kid and where does he live?"

"That was Harry Waldheim," one of the frightened rats responded.

"Where does he live?"

"38 Harmon Glen," another answered.

"Now I want all of you to leave. We have work to do," barked the man, regrouping.

But the fire was already out, and the tree house was just a pile of ashes. No real damage had been done to the forest. Harry hid and watched from a distance knowing he was invisible.

He spent the rest of the day silently creeping away from the scene of his crime, without food or water, often stopping to rest and drift and dream and listen. He could hear the droning buzz of cicadas and, in the distance, a bull dozer clearing yet another lot for yet another new home, encroaching further into his woods, into his private habitat.

It was getting late. After contemplating running away and living free and on his own in the woods forever, or maybe even killing himself, Harry, badly needed a bath, a glass of water and something to eat. He entered the rear door of his parents' house and ran into his mother, in her apron, washing the dinner dishes.

"Where have you been?"

Harry was silent.

"Don't you ignore me," she grunted and scrubbed even harder, trying to ignore him back.

He heard the muffled voices of two men in the living room.

"You have a visitor in the living room." Wiping her hands on her apron, she grabbed him by the shirt and shoved him through the door. His father and the firefighter stood talking.

"That's him," snarled the self-righteous volunteer, still holding Harry's torn collar in one hand, he pointed and shook his finger with the other. "I have a good mind to mop the floor with you."

"You owe this gentleman an apology. Lucky for you he has agreed to not press charges. Now apologize." His father looked at Harry's disheveled state with nothing but contempt and disgust.

Harry, exhausted, frail, filthy and starving, stared down at the floor. His eyes were red and moist but he remained silent.

"Harry...apologize. Now!" his seething father yelled.

Reluctantly, Harry mouthed, "Sorry..."

"What was that? We didn't hear you. Did you hear him?" his father asked his new friend and co-prosecutor.

"No. I guess I'll just have to write this up and book him," the smug fireman offered.

"Harry!" his father barked.

Only slightly louder, Harry whispered, "Sorry."

"Now apologize like you really mean it! Do you want to go to reform school?" Harry's father grabbed him, shook him and smacked him several times in the face and then on his ear. The room went silent, except for a ringing in the eight-year-old's skull. A trickle of blood ran from his nose and his lower lip, which was beginning to swell. He turned on his heels and spun out of the room. He ran upstairs to his bedroom. In spite of the ringing in his ears, he heard his father run up the stairs like a raging bull. In a moment, his father was on him, smacking and punching him while Harry lay on his back, kicking and screaming, trying to protect himself. Ultimately, he landed a direct kick to his maniac-of-a-father's left testicle. Everything went quiet until his father backed up, turned around and limped out of the room, defeated.

Several hours later, Harry was lying on his back, in bed, unwashed, unfed, and still wearing his collarless torn shirt. It was late and quiet and he was the only one awake. He looked out the window at the moon, through patches of clouds and the still branches of clustered grey birch trees. His face streaked with dried tears, he finally fell into a deep slumber amid the crescendo of the sounds of crickets and katydids.

On auto pilot, he found himself in Bucksport, only a few minutes from the Lipschitz house. Harry needed a moment. He pulled into a parking lot, got out of his car, on slightly shaky legs, and walked into the diner. He slid onto a stool at the counter as a waitress placed a menu and a glass of water in front of him. Picking up the glass, he turned his back to the counter, swiveling on the stool to observe the diner filled with loving families: mothers, fathers and children all squirming, talking and laughing with energy and enthusiasm. His eyes scanned the room slowly and the sounds around him seemed to slow down. It was a peaceful scene, yet highly animated. Families were hugging and touching and smiling. The place was filled with joy and an inexplicable lightness. He finished his water and left without ordering.

He pulled over to the side of the street just in front of the mailbox at number one Knoll N Gorge Drive. His old Ford blended in with the rest of the numerous contractors' trucks and vans lined up to service the surrounding McMansions. A road crew nearby was cutting apart a fallen tree and loading branches into a large chipper-shredder. Harry closed his eyes for a moment as he sat in his truck. He remembered the time, a week after he moved to New York City, when he went flying over the handlebars of his bicycle. A small block of wood had jammed between his spokes and the front forks, stopping him dead and in less than a second, shooting him headfirst into the pavement on 17th Street. He recalled the dream he had in that split second of falling. He was sitting by the swimming pool of his dear friends, the Stolls, on Shelter Island, drinking mint juleps. The air was perfect, the sun was perfect, everything was peaceful and perfect.

The memory dissipated as he opened his eyes to observe Mrs. Lipschitz—Sarah—and her three kids just pulling into the driveway. He watched as they got out of the black SUV, all smiling and laughing and horsing around: happy, like the people in the diner. He glanced toward the passenger seat, at the gun and the knife and the box filled with evidence. He tucked the Lugar, cop style, in the back of his pants, picked up the box and walked toward the house. The sound of the chipper-shredder was almost deafening as he passed, the crew continuing to shove branches into its wide mouth. No one noticed Harry. Their backs were turned to him as they concentrated on their work. In an instant, Harry lifted the box, filled with evidence, and tossed it into the mouth of the shredder. After a moment of loud grinding, the evidence was confetti, blasting up into the air, flying and floating through the neighborhood.

He ignored the protests of the road crew and continued walking toward the house. He stopped a few feet from the large white pine tree, just on the edge of the property. The sky was filled with shreds of paper and slivers of plastic, and the Lipschitz kids were running around in the yard catching bits and pieces. Sarah smiled at their game. Richard Lipschitz appeared from the back of the house on his riding mower, buried in his headphones, cigar in one hand, beer in the other, ignored by his family. He was oblivious to everything. Harry watched from a distance, unobserved. Then, slowly he backed away from the kids, the wife, and his mortal enemy.

Eyes closed, he moved unsteadily, slightly backward toward the giant white pine tree. Harry, now lighter than air, began to rise upward, toward a bright blue sky. The house, the kids, the mom and the strange little man on the riding mower appeared farther and farther away. The drone of internal combustion engines faded. He was high above the ground, nearing the top of the white pine.

The eight-year-old boy climbed higher and higher, finally reaching the highest tip of the tallest tree in the world.

Acknowledgments

Special thanks to all those who have convinced and encouraged me to continue moving forward with this seemingly endless project, and to my talented and extremely patient editor, D.L.K.

CPSIA information can be obtained
at www.ICGtesting.com
Printed in the USA
LVHW030416230221
679682LV00020B/833/J

9 781736 563519